Initiations

Barbara Winkes

ISBN: 978-1-0693045-1-3

Cover art © May Dawney Designs

Created with Atticus

For D.

Chapter One

There was no sign of Jordan or Kate when Ellie entered the *Night Shift*. In fact, there was nobody familiar, so she decided to take a seat at the bar and have a glass of wine while waiting for them. She was worried about her friend who had become quiet and withdrawn ever since a missing person case she had worked on turned into a homicide investigation.

This case was the reason why Jordan was late, too. Lately, Kate had expressed little interest in going out with friends after work. Since she stayed at Derek Henderson's most of the time, Ellie hardly saw her anymore outside of the precinct, even though they shared an apartment.

She handed a bill to the bartender who placed the glass of chilled wine in front of her.

"Hey. I almost didn't recognize you. Nice color."

The woman taking a seat on the stool next to hers looked different from the way Ellie remembered her, too, her blonde hair cut to chin length, her clothes more casual than she had ever seen her in.

"You're back."

"I see you found a new place," Dr. Bethany Roberts said. "Not quite the same. The *Code 7* was legendary, even though it was kind of...rustic."

"I'm surprised to see you here."

"Why, because I'm not one of the down-to-earth cops you usually hang with?" Bethany asked, amused. She ordered a whiskey on the rocks. "It's about work, but you already guessed that. At least I hope you did. How are you doing?"

Ellie shrugged, still somewhat perplexed about Bethany making small talk.

"I'm good. We've been good," she added with a hint of an edge. Defensive. That wasn't likely to go away around Bethany.

"That's great to hear."

"What's going on?" After half the glass, Ellie found she was brave enough to ask the question.

Bethany gave her a wry smile. "Honestly, I'm not sure, but I know this. You've seen me at my worst, and you're still polite. It's only fair to return the favor, don't you think?"

"I guess."

"Besides, I'm grateful. I was clinging to something that clearly wasn't worth holding on to. That's over. It's better for all of us."

Ellie took another sip, uncomfortable with where this conversation was going. She never knew how to pick the right tone with Bethany, or what she expected her to say at this moment. *Don't worry, you'll find someone?* Maybe she could come up with something less condescending.

"Is this about Deane? The A.D.A. has charged him."

"Esposito, yes. I'm sure he's guilty of something, but with him, we're only scratching the surface. I shouldn't be telling you this, though I'm sure you are up to date on the case. How are you getting along with her?"

"The A.D.A? I don't have much to do with her. I know she worked here before, but that's all."

It was Bethany's turn to look surprised. "Jordan didn't tell you?"

"Tell me what?"

"Oh, nothing. I thought you knew. It's really not that important—forget I said anything."

"What did you mean? I'm asking you politely."

"You know you weren't the only one, right? The difference is you won. After her, I was still fooling myself into thinking that there was something we could fix. Never mind, with the way Jordan left her, there's not much of a chance Valerie came back for her. And that's all you're getting from me on that subject. It's not one I'm happy to revisit."

You brought it up, Ellie wanted to say, unsure how to feel about the news. Jordan hadn't mentioned her previous involvement with the A.D.A. She'd had more than enough opportunities.

"Then let's not. What did you mean that we're only scratching the surface with Deane?"

"Really? I'm supposed to save the fun stuff for the meeting tomorrow. Maybe Bristol lets you come. You're still going to take the detective's exam?"

"I haven't changed any plans," Ellie said. She hoped Jordan hadn't either. "I'll ask him."

"Yes, you do that. Oh, and here's the gang. Like old times."

Jordan walked in with a group of other detectives from the precinct, Derek Henderson, Maria Doss, and Cliff Waters. Ellie was relieved to see Kate with Derek. She slipped off the barstool and went to greet Jordan with a kiss, the second glass of wine sparking more public display of affection than usual.

"Hello to you too," Jordan said with a surprised laugh. "You really missed me."

They found themselves a table at the far end of the bar. Ellie would have liked to confront her sins of omission right now, but to her dismay, Valerie Esposito entered the bar. She was heading for their table, but realizing Bethany had joined them, she turned and stayed at the counter.

"I so did," Ellie admitted as she sat down next to Jordan, ignoring Bethany studying their exchange with an amused expression.

"I assume neither of you missed *me* much, but here it goes. Tomorrow, 7:00 a.m. in the conference room. I guess your boss told you that we'll take Deane into federal custody."

"What?" Jordan said, obviously not happy with this turn of events.

"I know, you never were a morning person, sorry about that. We'll have to wrap this up quickly."

"I wasn't talking about the time. This is a murder investigation. There's no reason for you to be on it."

"Oh, wait for it, there is," Bethany insisted. "I'll have to wait until tomorrow, though, because then Valerie has no choice whether or not to join us. We'll all do our jobs. You'll see it will be just fine."

"Whatever," Jordan dismissed her. "Is anybody going to get drinks?"

"I'll go," Derek offered. "Kate?"

"I'll have a beer."

"I'll have another glass of wine," Ellie said simultaneously.

Bethany swirled the rest of her whiskey in the glass where the ice cubes had almost melted down. Derek hadn't waited for her. "A warm welcome as usual. How could I ever stay away?"

She hadn't been so wrong, Ellie thought. She had stayed polite as much as she could, given the circumstances, because she didn't believe in vilifying professional and powerful women. Still, she resented Bethany for stirring up trouble with such glee. Although—there didn't have to be trouble, right? If Jordan hadn't mentioned it, this episode belonged in the past. That's where they'd leave it.

The initial plan had been to make it an early night and stay at Ellie's apartment, since it was closer to town. Ellie had trouble letting go of the conversation with Bethany, even though the conclusion was obvious: She had won. Jordan was here with her. She wanted her. That was all that mattered, right?

Ellie knew that Jordan had cheated on Bethany before during their long-term relationship. It wasn't up to her to forgive the incident or obsess about it. She hadn't brought it up in the early days, because whatever was happening between them, seemed so fragile...Then, a lot happened within the span of weeks that made them take a hard look at their priorities, and they had found it was each other.

So far, so good?

"What's on your mind?" Jordan asked, a soft whisper against her neck, while Jordan's hands were wandering across her body, familiar territory.

"Nothing. Except you, of course." That wasn't even a lie, but Jordan sat back and studied her curiously.

"For some reason, I don't like it when Bethany catches you alone."

"What, you're worried about the things she could tell me? We're past that. At least I thought we were."

"What's that supposed to mean?" Jordan's tone wasn't defensive, simply inquiring. Ellie wished she knew a way to bring this conversation to a halt and bring them back to where they'd been moments ago. She had no illusions.

"All right. A.D.A. Esposito? Why didn't you tell me you two had...something, a while ago?"

"What?" Jordan shook her head with a bemused laugh. "I wasn't aware we were doing full disclosure listing all of our exes."

"Not all of them. Just the ones we might run into on a regular basis."

"Then we're okay on my side. Can we put this to rest now?"

Ellie was tired and still a bit tipsy, not the best circumstances to press the subject. At the moment, she also lacked caution—and part of her felt slightly offended by the insinuation that only one of them seemed to attract gorgeous, tempting women walking in and out of her life.

"You still didn't answer my question. Why didn't you tell me when she came back—if it means nothing?"

"Jesus, the woman spent years in my head. There's no need for her to get into yours too." Jordan got up and started to dress.

"Where are you going?"

"I'm going home. I'd like to catch some sleep before the meeting tomorrow—even though we all know how it's going to turn out."

"Jordan. Come on. You remember it's a half hour drive as opposed to five minutes from here? Besides, you had a couple of drinks."

"Speak for yourself. I had one beer. Good night, Ellie."

"Could you please wait...?"

By the time Ellie had put on a robe and opened the door to the hallway, Jordan was gone. Kate and Derek sat in the kitchen, pretending they hadn't witnessed the scene.

"What are you looking at?" Ellie wasn't in the mood to indulge their pretense.

"I better go too," Derek said, getting up. "See you, Ellie."

"Yeah," she muttered, walking to the fridge where there was still a half-empty bottle of wine. "Don't say anything," she warned Kate who shrugged.

"I wasn't going to. Give me a glass, too, and tell me what's up. You've been acting strange."

Ellie poured each of them a glass and sat down across from Kate. "Bethany told me that Jordan and Esposito were..." What exactly? A couple? For how long?

"Oh. I see, but that was a while ago, right? Do you think there's still something?"

"I don't know. I don't think so. But if it's irrelevant, why not answer a simple question?"

"Maybe it was painful? Sometimes it's a good idea to just be with the person you're with, you know what I mean?"

"I'm sorry."

Her situation differed greatly from Kate's. Her friend was in a new relationship after her fiancé had been killed in the line of duty. It was hardly something you could compare to the jealousy Ellie wasn't proud to feel—but she did.

"No need, just friendly advice. I thought you were doing great."

"We were. We are. This just took me by surprise."

"It's understandable. Tomorrow will be better."

"Yeah. I hope so. Thanks for the pep talk."

Kate smiled wistfully. "Any time. I'm going to bed now. Rogers asked me to come to the meeting as well."

"Oh, really? That's...good."

"Yeah. I realize that is the only thing I can do for Jennifer and her mother now."

"Have a good night," Ellie said. She went into the bathroom where she sat on the edge of the tub, tired, on the verge of crying for no good reason.

She was good at planning, Jordan had said so.

She had wanted Jordan, and a career, and she had made both happen, but she felt like all those accomplishments might be in danger. She should be in that meeting, as she was planning to take the detective's exam soon. Sergeant Bristol seemed to have no problem with Kate attending. Of course, she had worked with Detective Rogers during the search for Jennifer Beaumont. Ellie, however, would have to ask, and it wasn't even clear if he'd say yes.

Jordan—she wasn't going to lose her after everything they'd been through together. She was simply frustrated to see her getting testy over this subject. Ellie understood getting testy, and impatient, with something trivial. She understood Jordan needed room to work through the latest upheavals in her life, but damn it, Ellie's life had been disrupted too, by getting abducted and kept in the dark for days. Literally, and then as to her kidnappers' intentions.

She didn't want to go back there, think about it. She did pretty well distracting herself when Jordan was sleeping beside her. Obviously, that wasn't an option tonight.

Chapter Two

After being awake for the better part of the night, Ellie overslept the next morning and would have been tragically late if Kate hadn't woken her. There was no time for breakfast, especially if she wanted to try and have a word with the sergeant. Kate hadn't eaten either, and the ride to the department was a silent and pensive one.

Ellie knocked on Sergeant Bristol's door minutes before the meeting, hoping she wouldn't sound too desperate when making her case. She would sort out things with Jordan later. This was important. Maybe her interest wasn't completely unselfish as Kate's, and she wanted to stay close on a case that involved both Bethany Roberts and Valerie Esposito. Maybe the sergeant wouldn't want to invest more personnel in a case that was now mostly in the hands of the Feds. Well, they would be calling the shots anyway, and if they needed anything, from files to officers, they'd get it. Ellie had to make sure she'd be on the front line of this.

Bristol listened to her, to Ellie's surprise not even arguing.

"Go ahead. Marshall will ride with Lyons today."

"Thank you, sir." She waited, unsure how she'd managed so quickly.

"I'll be there in ten minutes. If you'll excuse me now."

"Of course."

She hurried to the conference room where, to Ellie's dismay, everyone except her boss was already gathered, all eyes on her as she entered the room. The lieutenant was conversing with a male agent. Ellie remembered having seen him before. His name was Russo. Derek sat on the far end of the table, leaning back in his chair comfortably, Kate and Detective Rogers next to him.

Bethany stood behind the desk, working on her laptop in preparation of a power point presentation. Next to Jordan sat Valerie Esposito. Ellie suppressed a sigh. Now was not the time to worry—or be petty. She pulled herself a chair across from Jordan the moment Sergeant Bristol entered the room.

"We're complete, great," Bethany observed. "Good morning, ladies and gentlemen. Let's begin."

If all these women could stay professional despite their history with one another, so could Ellie, right?

"The reason we have a special interest in Raphael Deane is his family. He appears to have been estranged from them, but his involvement with Jennifer Beaumont shows he could have been in touch."

"Involvement? He murdered her," Jordan muttered.

"I don't doubt that," Bethany said. "We still need him. This is a chance for us to prosecute and prevent a number of crimes committed by his family. We believe that some of them go back decades, and there is likely a relation to a couple of cold cases—unsolved disappearances, possible homicides. We have the files here, and we'll need you to familiarize yourself with those cases."

"Who are they?" Henderson asked. "The mafia?"

"Not quite. Before we get to that in depth, I'd like to go back to the Beaumont case for a moment. Officer McCarthy?"

"Her mother came to the station to report her missing," Kate supplied. "Jennifer lived in Iowa where she went to college and met Raphael Deane while he was visiting his uncle Jeremiah.

She came home for her aunt's funeral. She got on the plane, got a rental, and Raphael Deane caught up to her in the parking lot. We later found that he'd asked one of his friends to bring back the car to the rental office. He..." She swallowed hard. "Killed her and dumped her body in a landfill. He said it was because she pulled away from him, refused to obey him. There was no evidence of rape, but then again, the scene was extremely contaminated as you can imagine, and he did talk about teaching her a lesson."

Russo looked a bit sick.

"Deane's father and two uncles call themselves the Prophets of Better Days," Bethany continued. "They set up camp in three different states, ours included. They've been clever, preparing this for decades, buying real estate, establishing themselves as a church and finally, getting politically involved."

"A religious cult, then?" Again, all eyes were on Ellie. "What does this have to do with Deane and the murder?"

She saw realization dawn on Jordan's face.

"The clothes and the hair...that looks like something women would wear in this context. So she was one of them?"

"She lived on the compound in Iowa but then left abruptly without asking permission. That's what we hear from the Better Days folks there. They all swear they didn't know she was leaving."

"Earlier, she sent her mother back a piece of jewelry that meant a lot to her, her grandmother's," Kate remembered.

"Yeah, they're not supposed to wear any sort of jewelry, which goes only for the women, of course. I believe sending it back was more of a cry for help. Her mother knew something wasn't right and contacted the police, but it was already too late. Not only do we think Raphael was sent to intercept Jennifer Beaumont, but he was supposed to bring her back. It's highly significant that when you found her, she was wearing the signature clothes for women in the Better Days cult."

"You think the family told him to kill her?" Jordan asked.

"It's possible. Either way, this could be our chance to get much deeper. There have been rumors of child abuse, child labor, and domestic violence. So far, no one's been willing to testify. We haven't been able to place somebody undercover either. It is almost impossible to get to them as most of the women are so indoctrinated and scared that they won't say anything."

"Beaumont got away, if only for a little while. She didn't tell anyone about what she saw?"

"Not that we know of."

Esposito nodded. "We tried to prosecute a case a couple of years ago. It quickly went nowhere. They have politicians in their pockets, align with influential people."

"So we just let them go on?" Ellie couldn't help it.

"Not exactly," Russo said. "We'll have to convince Raphael to reach out to his family, his father Daniel in particular, and tell them he has someone interested in the group. This is tricky. Beaumont was an exception—they don't often take new recruits, because according to their manifesto, they are already too 'poisoned' by the outside."

"Lovely," Jordan said. "How are you getting your man in?"

"Figure of speech, I hope." Bethany leaned against the desk. "It should be a woman."

"Why? Doesn't it make more sense for men being interested in that lifestyle?"

Derek shot Jordan a quizzical look in response to her question.

Ellie thought of recent conversations with her ex Rhonda who had briefly dated Raphael Deane. What if...?

"They are on edge, with Raphael's arrest. They'd be more inclined to believe a woman, if she says all the right lines. And we need him to introduce her."

"I'm not sure how this can work," Jordan said. "If they are letting him take the fall, why would they do anything for him?"

Ellie had the same question, but Bethany had an answer prepared for them. "If killing Beaumont was some sort of test, Raphael passed. For the family to continue business as usual, they need to act all outraged about the 'black sheep,' but they can turn around and be all about forgiveness the next moment if he offers them remorse and dangles a prize in front of them they can't resist. If it all works out, we can work with A.D.A. Esposito on a deal."

Valerie nodded. "I'm not happy about it, but if that means we finally get them, I'll take it."

"What are you saying?" Ellie flinched as Kate jumped to her feet.

"Officer McCarthy." Bristol's tone was level but held a clear warning.

"He murdered her, possibly raped her too. I saw the body. How can we make any sort of deal with scum like him?"

"I understand your feelings," Bethany said softly. "Unfortunately, he has something we want: Access. That has the potential to change the lives of many women and children. I believe Jennifer was about to talk. She wanted whatever she saw out in the open, and we'll best do our job by respecting that wish."

She was good, Ellie had to give her that.

"You all know that Rhonda Marks came in to tell us about Raphael Deane in the first place," she said. "She knows him, didn't quite understand his intentions, but she gave us a first hint of something bizarre going on. What if I could make the contact—"

"Ellie," Jordan said sharply. "Stop it right there. I'm sure what Dr. Roberts is meaning to say is that she already chose someone for the job."

"I'm sorry, Officer Harding, but that's right." Bethany frowned. "Agent Strickland should be here right now. I'm not sure..."

"I'm here, I'm here. Sorry. My cab got stuck in traffic and it was either wait it out or walk. In which case I wouldn't be here yet."

Ellie was quite sure that Jordan wasn't going to let her off the hook yet, but everyone else's attention was on the agent who had just entered the room. Upon a first impression, she looked younger than Ellie, which bothered her.

She had brought them Rhonda who could identify two of Deane's friends, so they could catch him. She was ready to step up, and Bethany knew her.

The psychiatrist regarded the younger woman with something akin to indulgent affection.

"Meet Agent Strickland. Raphael Deane will introduce her to the family."

"How do you know this will work?" Jordan asked, still sounding frustrated. "You said they don't trust anyone, hardly ever take in anyone from the outside. Why do you think he will help us?"

"Because he has no choice. I read his confession. There's hardly anything to sugar-coat that he killed Beaumont, and A.D.A. Esposito is ready to go for the maximum penalty. Given that kind of choice, most people reconsider their loyalty to the family."

"What if he doesn't?"

"We can always go back to Officer Harding's connections, but that would be a last resort."

Jordan's expression said that she was more than grateful.

"Then let's make sure it doesn't come to that."

"How are you planning to do this? I assume the Bureau will be responsible," the lieutenant remarked.

"This is a joint operation now," Russo said. "Deane knows he's isolated from his family's influence. We're giving him a chance. He'd be crazy not to take it."

"The thing is, he already is crazy, but let's say you can convince him, what's going to happen next?"

"I'm certain we will convince him, and Agent Strickland is ready," Bethany said with confidence. "Thank you, Lieutenant, for providing us with the resources. We appreciate it."

Ellie had followed the exchange with disappointment, then excitement, for being a part of this, until she saw Kate's expression. She instantly felt guilty—and all of that before she had a chance to talk to Jordan. This would not be easy.

There was no time to catch up with Ellie before Jordan followed Valerie, Bethany, and the other agents to the interrogation room. She and Derek stayed outside in the observation area with Valerie and Agent Russo. Jordan wondered if this was the smart decision. Deane clearly didn't believe in female authority of any kind—she had seen her share of that.

At the moment, her thoughts were drifting slightly, to the pointless argument with Ellie, her knee-jerk reaction of removing herself from it. She had been ready to apologize this morning, but then Ellie came up with the idea of offering herself as bait.

By now, Jordan knew that every now and then, she needed to take leaps, not steps forward, and that she was willing to take a risk, but this was going too far. Thank God Bethany didn't feel the need to prove something to either of them. Lilah

Strickland was young, granted, but she had field experience, and had studied the Prophets of Better Days for a long time. Besides, only small details wavered—men who believed in a patriarchal society were usually pretty easy to decipher.

Jordan was aware that her thoughts were going in contradicting directions. She simply didn't want Ellie on the front line of this, no matter how good it might be for her career. If that was selfish, then so be it. With the history of this group, Raphael Deane might not have been the first to commit a murder.

"Mr. Deane. Agent Strickland and I would like to talk to you about the options you have from here. We know about your family, and we have some important questions."

Deane's gaze rested on Strickland for a long time before he looked at Bethany. "You'll have to ask them, then. I did my part. I told the police I did it."

"True, but I don't think this was all your plan. We hear that you were supposed to bring Jennifer back into the fold. I assume she was resisting."

"I killed her. Then I panicked and tried to think of a way to get rid of the body. I put her in a garbage bag and drove her to the landfill. That's all. It has nothing to do with my family."

"That's what you said, Raphael."

He scoffed, obviously unhappy with Bethany addressing him with his first name.

"Frankly, it doesn't look good for you. Killing a woman in cold blood because you don't agree with the way she lives her life won't get you any sympathy from the jury. You're making it very easy for the prosecutor."

"Aren't you happy, bitch?" he asked in a scathing voice.

Bethany regarded him with a small, amused smile until he looked away.

"We are curious about your father and uncles. You tell us everything we want to know—we might be able to help each other."

"I don't know what you want from me. Those are honorable men, taking their rightful places as head of the family. I know it's something that is mocked and dismissed on the outside, this is why we keep to ourselves."

"And the women know their place too?" There was an edge to Bethany's voice. Jordan admired her self-restraint at this moment. "That is, if they don't, you show them?"

"I thought you had questions." He grinned. "You already know everything."

"There's a lot that we don't know," Strickland said, sitting across from him. "I've been interested in the Prophets for a long time. You get them to open the door for me, and A.D.A. Esposito might go a little easier on you."

Deane shook his head. "I told you, I wasn't acting on their behalf. Why do you think I could get them to do anything for me? They haven't even sent a lawyer yet. I assume my father and uncles are angry at me, and I can't blame them. This, getting attention, leads to their names being smeared all over again."

"So you care," Lilah Strickland said softly. "Either way, the sooner you help us, the sooner their names will be out of the headlines. I imagine that's motivation for you. Let's face the facts. You're looking at life without parole at the very best, and that's not even a given. This offer isn't going to stand indefinitely. You get me on the inside, and they'll bring it down to life with the possibility of parole."

"I'd advise you to talk to your lawyer. You have two hours," Bethany announced. "After that, you're on your own."

"You are not qualified," he seethed. "You are unable to see their greatness."

"Well, you have the chance to educate us. We'll be back."

17

Bethany left the room, and Strickland followed her.

Jordan still questioned the wisdom of sending her into the lion's den, but in any case, it wouldn't be Ellie. That was the good news. Now she had to find her before Deane would come to any sort of conclusion—she still had to apologize.

Ellie was on her phone in the break room, ending the call when Jordan came inside.

"Hey. Do you have a moment?"

"Sure," Ellie said cautiously. "Did he take the deal?"

"Not yet. They gave him two hours."

"Okay." Ellie turned to the vending machine to get a coffee and a chocolate bar. Silence ensued for a few uncomfortable moments.

"Look, I'm sorry. I honestly didn't think we needed to discuss this. It's awkward enough to be working together."

"You think?" Ellie spun around, nearly spilling her coffee. "It's awkward for me, too, when everyone knows except me." She looked tired. "I don't want to fight with you. I love you."

"Same here."

"I wish you had told me, that's all."

"I made some bad choices," Jordan acknowledged. "I know that. You know it too. I don't like to be reminded of them all the time, and so...I took the easy way out. I'm sorry. Can we talk about what you offered earlier? I'd appreciate it if you shared something big like that with me first."

"Because you always share the big, important things?" Ellie picked up her chocolate bar. "I'm sorry. This is not the right moment. I understand what you're talking about, I really do, but this is my career. I need to make those decisions. You don't check with me every time you're about to go into a situation that might be dangerous, and I don't ask you to even though I wish I could. I worry about you, but I can't stop you from doing your job. That's a dilemma I'll have to live with, and I guess the same goes for you."

When Jordan didn't say anything, she went to leave the room.

"Ellie, wait."

Ellie carefully set down her coffee and snack and let herself be embraced. The moment didn't last long, as Lilah Strickland entered the room with a cheery "There you are. I've been sent to get you—Deane and his lawyer have come to a conclusion. You don't want to miss the fun."

That was mostly meant for Jordan, but Ellie obviously had a few more minutes to spare.

❦

The public defender was sweating, and they soon learned it was not a good sign for any of them.

"I don't think any one of you understands the meaning of loyalty," Raphael Deane said. "I will not betray my family. I know what you're after, and you're not going to get it, disrupting the peace of our community."

"This is ridiculous, and you know it," Bethany told him. "You think they'll be looking after you? You said it yourself, they didn't send a lawyer. On the other hand, I'm sure your attorney has told you you're making a big mistake."

"By not ratting out those closest to me? No. You can lock me up forever, or kill me, for all I care. The Prophets and their legacy will live on, and you can't stop them. They are only getting more powerful each day."

The megalomaniac rhetoric was giving Jordan a headache. She found it chilling, wondering how many weapons there were on each of the compounds, and if an apocalyptic vision was part of their plan. Of course. It always was.

There was already too much craziness out there that went unchecked, indulged. Usually, women and children were the ones to suffer.

"I tried to convince my client, and informed him about all the possibilities," the attorney said. "He is unwilling to cooperate."

"I can see that," Bethany muttered. "I'm sorry to hear that, Mr. Deane. This is out of our hands now."

Jordan could tell she was feeling defeated. She knew from experience that Bethany didn't take that feeling well—she had to talk to her as soon as possible. They could bring back Rhonda Marks, and the friends she'd met while dating him, try to find any other former members of the Better Days cult. She would do what she could to make sure Ellie wouldn't go near any of them.

They reconvened in the conference room shortly after.

"Damn it," Bethany cursed. "I was sure he'd take the deal."

"Now what, back to the drawing table?" Jordan asked.

"I'd like to speak to those friends, Ellen Slater, Dwayne Whitman, and Rhonda Marks. Meanwhile, Lilah can work with Officer Harding and bring her up to speed. I need an officer to go over their websites, see if anything clicks."

"Why not me?" Kate asked. "I was first to talk to Mrs. Beaumont..."

"We're all right here, Officer McCarthy," Bethany said. "You may see Sergeant Bristol. Thank you," she added with a pointed look when Kate was about to open her mouth to protest.

"Now, Agent Strickland, Officer Harding, get a room and get started on this. Let's bring those friends here."

"I already called Rhonda," Ellie said with a look to Jordan that was more defensive than apologetic.

"Great. Then we can all get to work. Detectives Rogers and Carpenter, and Henderson, please come with me. I have the information on those cases we're looking into."

Bethany was in the mode she liked best: Telling everyone what to do.

⁂

"This is exciting," Agent Strickland said. "It's the first time I'm on a multi-departmental task force like this. Gives me more of an idea how the local precincts work."

Ellie nodded and smiled, not wanting to be impolite, though she wasn't in the mood for small talk. Maybe this was just a streak of bad luck—if that was the case, she hoped it would go away soon.

There wasn't much to learn from the Better Days websites. Comments were strictly moderated, and so the people who were accepted were those who believed in the lifestyle: Men as the head of the household, women as their submissive. It would have angered and frustrated her on the best of days, but she was far from having a good day. She understood Bethany's hope for making this a bigger case than the murder of Jennifer Beaumont. With Deane being uncooperative, they were on a tight schedule.

He was the murderer, no doubt about it, but they still didn't know if he had acted on someone else's orders. A couple of cold cases that might or might not be related. Meanwhile, there were newer cases in Homicide, and it was only a matter of time before the lieutenant would remind everyone of their urgency.

That didn't include the current strain on her relationship with Jordan. She wanted to go home and crawl under a blanket. Of course, that was not an option. Ellie knew she was lucky to get exactly the spot she'd hoped for, working with someone from Bethany's team.

This was probably the only bright spot—they had a common goal, and for that, each of them could put their differences and petty feelings aside.

"It's messy," Lilah tried again. "The problem is, they are secretive about what's happening on the inside, and they are in bed with some powerful people. Makes you wonder how many bosses and politicians want to keep women on a leash."

"Too many," Ellie muttered. She had always thought that men like Darby, or Josh Ward, were only the extreme of something dangerously ingrained in society. Boys will be boys. Men could take whatever they want. "My friend put in lots of hours with missing persons," she said. "Maybe it's better that we don't get to sweeten the deal for Deane. Either way, he's a killer."

Lilah regarded her curiously. "Sure, but we have to find a way. Any way. They keep children hostage from their mothers if they don't obey the rules. A bunch of grey-haired old white men tell them what to do every day in their lives, and Raphael? He's not smart enough to come up with a murder plan. You don't panic and then try to get rid of the body like that. Someone told him what to do."

"Aren't you scared?"

Ellie wanted to slap her hand against her mouth. This wasn't what she'd meant to ask, though her question confronted her with an uncomfortable truth. She might usually forge ahead, but that was her way of dealing with fear. Fear that there were too many of them, coming out of the woodwork every time they put one of them away. To her relief, Lilah didn't seem to think she was silly to ask.

"Oh, I'm terrified. No agent has ever been on the inside. They have a rigorous vetting process, which makes it even more interesting that Jennifer was accepted so quickly, and that she had time to go back to college, contact her mom and even try to come home. Punishment wasn't as swift as you would expect."

"Why? Did Raphael rebel against it? He did have some feelings for her after all?"

"I'm not sure if he has real feelings for anyone." Lilah shrugged. "In any case, it will not be easy. But it's important. Yes, there are others like that, but if we could shut down Jeremiah and his crew, it would be a big step."

"For sure. And you couldn't find anyone willing to testify against them?"

"The case A.D.A. Esposito mentioned, it fell apart quickly. They have their intimidation tactics—but that's the problem, it's all rumors and innuendo. We need this break badly."

"You know that my ex was dating him for a while. Certainly, we can't send her in, but I could try to talk to him," Ellie mused. "We didn't understand it right away when she told us about him. Now it makes sense—he was trying to influence her, change her hair and clothes. Maybe he thought he could save her." She couldn't help the shudder, thinking of what Deane's efforts had done to Jennifer Beaumont.

"Yeah, it's a good thing he didn't get to try," Lilah said, sensing where Ellie's thoughts had been going. "It's worth a shot. Let's ask Dr. Roberts when we're done here."

At least someone around here was open to her ideas.

Chapter Three

J ordan wasn't too happy about Bethany's disclosures to Ellie, but none of that mattered at the moment. No matter how many times they talked to Raphael Deane's friends, Dwayne, Ellen and Rhonda Marks, they always got the same answers. He was a bit weird. Judging women on the way they dressed all the time. He didn't talk about his family, ever. They remembered hearing something about the Prophets in the news a long time ago, but it was all vague.

When they decided to take a break for a moment, Jordan got herself a coffee and, on second thought, brought one for Bethany. There was no need for high school antics. They were all grown-ups. They were all better off now.

She understood Bethany's frustration better than anyone else, after barely escaping with her life from a man who thought he had the right and the calling to teach women "morals." When Bethany had involved Ellie in the case after her abduction, it had helped her, and for that, Jordan was grateful.

That was a lot of justification for a cup of coffee, she reflected.

Bethany accepted the cup with a wistful smile.

"Thanks. It's not all that bad here. I think your coffee is one of the reasons I like to come back—it's certainly not for the welcome, or the amazing progress. Damn. I need this to work."

"We all hope it will. It's going to be hard to prove their involvement with those cold cases though."

"Tell me something I don't know." Bethany sighed. "It's ironic, isn't it, you, me, Esposito on this case."

"If you say so."

"Hey, I'm sorry. I was sure Ellie knew about her. It seemed to me that you were pretty honest with her, and so quickly. I thought by now you'd have planned your wedding." She laughed, putting her cup on the windowsill. "No, I'm not as bitter as this sounds. I've had my time to mourn and resent you both for a while. Besides, I might not be in town for much longer."

"What does that mean?"

"There might be an opportunity, but I know this case has to pan out for The Powers That Be to even consider me. I really want this."

"I think we all want for these people to be held accountable. You can be sure everyone's on your side."

"Yeah, except for your partner. He still hates me."

"Derek hates very few people, and believe me, you're not one of them." That might stretch the truth a bit, Jordan was aware.

"Thanks for trying. I need you guys on this as long as possible. I know they murdered these women. If we can't prove it, all I have is a bunch of jerks getting off on their patriarchal fantasies, and women who indulge them. If they are coerced, we can never prove that. I'm not willing to accept that, and neither is Agent Strickland."

"She's young. Does she have the experience to pull this off?"

"You're asking me because Harding offered herself? I'm sure she could do it though. She's cute enough for them to think she's harmless, and her record so far is pretty impressive."

"Don't go there. Ever."

"Well, at this moment, no one's going anywhere, unfortunately, but to answer your question: Yes. Strickland has what it takes, and we need to find a way to get her on the inside. She is our best bet."

Jordan had detected something else in Bethany's tone, and her expression must have shown her surprise.

"Okay, now get your mind out of the gutter. I'm not a cradle robber. Besides, she has a husband and a young child...and I'm seeing someone. My age."

"Good for you. I'm sorry for assuming—"

There was a knock on the door, preceding Ellie and Agent Strickland walking into the room.

"Did you find anything?" Bethany asked.

"I'm afraid there's nothing of use on their websites," Strickland said. "Officer Harding had an idea that's worth listening to, I think."

⁘

While Jordan was still fairly uneasy about the idea, she had to admit that it was worth a try. A monitored conversation with Deane was far from what Ellie had suggested earlier.

Ellie seemed relieved about her lack of protest. She walked into the interrogation room with a confidence that shouldn't have surprised Jordan, but it did, and she felt instantly bad about it. She and Bethany stayed in the observation area with Agent Strickland.

"What is this now? You're going to try to get me to testify against my people too? Pathetic."

"I'm here about Rhonda. I'm a friend of hers."

"What about Rhonda?" he asked.

"She wanted to know how you are doing. She can't visit you at the moment, so she asked me to see you."

"Why would she care? She was never that interested in my opinion anyway."

"Maybe because she didn't understand. You were critical of her, but she thinks you might have had a point. That you wanted to help her. She misses you."

"I tried to help her all right, but you wouldn't understand."

"Well...I'm on my break now, so I have some time. Why don't you try?"

"Rhonda didn't understand the first thing about modesty. Why would you? You think you can walk down the street in your short skirts and high heels, exposing your bodies, and there will be no consequences?"

"Did you ever talk to her about consequences? What are they anyway? You harass women? Rape them?"

"Those are the choices *they* make!" he yelled.

Ellie flinched slightly, but she didn't shrink back.

"Her ex was really lucky," Bethany said, and Jordan nodded, still both intrigued and spooked by seeing this side of Ellie. She'd been right. She had to find her own path, and Jordan couldn't hold her back while dealing with her own issues. They had agreed not to go too fast, but at the moment, Bethany's remark in mind, Jordan wondered if they had slowed down their progress for no good reason. They still had separate apartments.

"So that's why you killed Jennifer, because you didn't like the choices she made? Who told you that those were bad choices? I think Rhonda will be interested in that answer too."

He looked around, appearing nervous all of a sudden. "Is she here? Can she hear this? That was something completely different. I would have never touched her. Rhonda shut up and didn't ask questions when I told her not to. Don't you get it? Jenny was going to drag all of us into the dirt, smear our names. She was going to write a book full of lies. Somebody had to stop her. I didn't know what else to do!"

Jordan saw the startled look on Ellie's face when he started to cry.

"You know, moments like this, I can almost completely forgive her," Bethany said. "Look what she just did. No one ever said anything about a book. Now follow up on that, girl."

"I don't think you mentioned a book before," Ellie said as if she'd been able to hear her. "How did you know about it?"

"I found it on her computer. I deleted it, but she laughed at me, saying there would be more copies."

"There are no copies," Bethany muttered. "You guys have been through her phone, tablet, laptop...right?"

"There was nothing," Jordan said. She, too, felt a lot more hopeful about the case with this turn of events. "If such a copy still exists, it has probably names, dates...pretty much everything you dream of."

"Oh, I don't plan on just dreaming. We're going to nail him and the rest of this sorry bunch."

"You want to go in?"

"No. Let's give her a few more minutes. This ex sure has been helpful for our cause."

They turned their attention back to the scene behind the two-way mirror.

"Where would those be?" Ellie asked. "Did she mention anything, a safe deposit box maybe?"

"If I knew, do you think I'd tell you? Those were all lies. Fiction. I didn't want anyone to find them, but now that no one will, I don't see the harm in telling you. You can pass that on to Rhonda."

"I will tell her. Thanks for talking to me, Raphael. I appreciate it."

"Could you do me a favor?" he asked.

"I'm not sure about that, but it depends. What is it?"

"Could you check if someone else tried to see me? I don't trust the other cops, or this sad excuse for a lawyer."

"I'll check that and let you know," Ellie said.

"Wow, she's really good," Lilah Strickland commented.

"Yes, she is," Bethany confirmed, leaving Jordan with the uncomfortable feeling that this wasn't the last time Ellie got to have a conversation with Jennifer Beaumont's murderer.

She knew exactly how it felt—exhilarating when you realized you had them, tricked them into making a connection. That same connection could make you feel like crap afterwards, because if you built a good rapport with a killer, what did that make you?

She had to stop thinking like this, be more supportive of Ellie's career, when she certainly made no compromises in her own. It wouldn't be easy when at the same time, she wanted to protect her.

⁂

"Good job," Bethany commented when Ellie emerged from the interrogation room. Jordan gave her an appreciative nod too in case Ellie needed it from another source.

"We still don't know where that book is—or if it exists at all."

"You did good." Bethany wasn't convinced otherwise. "I'm sure he told the truth about the book—I'm less sure that he doesn't know where it is. Let him stew a little, go back later today and tell him that no one asked for him. He'll have to come to terms with the fact that no one will, so maybe he'll be inclined to tell us more. Jordan, you're up to date with the cold cases?"

"I am."

Those files made for a chilling read.

Delilah James and Eileen Yates had little in common at first sight: Delilah had been twenty-one when she disappeared, a wife, a mother of a young child. Eileen Yates was a thirteen-year-old runaway who had exchanged the foster home for the streets.

Then, the lines of their stories seemed to cross with one man, the founder of the Prophets of Better Days: Jeremiah Deane's family had gone to the same church as Delilah James, before he and his brothers Daniel—Raphael's father—and John created their own. The last sign of life from Eileen had been when she showed up at a mission connected to said church. This was where Jeremiah had worked prior to calling himself a prophet, and he had been questioned. He admitted to knowing Delilah from church and, half a year later, having seen Eileen, fifteen at the time, at the mission. He had criticized the latter in colorful terms.

"I don't think they prided themselves in rescuing a young woman off the street," Jordan said, referring to Eileen's file. "The language he used for her was pretty awful."

"No, that wasn't their intention at all. They needed young women to start their cult."

Jordan had had the same thoughts, though it sounded chillingly dystopian when put into words like that. It had been sixteen, respectively seventeen years ago that these women vanished. To think of what might have happened to them, and possibly others...Those were the days on the edge of a moment when she wanted to quit, let someone else deal with the ugliness, but she never would. She had to accept that Ellie was the same.

"Why Delilah, though? She had a family."

"She was also dating Jeremiah's oldest son before she got married. From what I understand, he was never questioned, because he was out of the country at the time of her disappearance and didn't come back until years after."

"So, they kidnap women at random, and then what?" Ellie asked. "I can't believe this is still happening. How did they pull this off?"

"Once you pull the wool over people's eyes, slap the label of religion on something, there are many, too many people who are willing to look the other way. They are a tightly knit group, and they allow no straying from the herd. This is why Raphael is without one of their high-priced lawyers now—he might have done exactly what they asked him for, but I assume this is still punishment for trying to break away in the first place. He must have had a reason, and if we find it, everything will unravel. Ellie, I need you to be his friend. His very good friend. Can you do that?"

Without a second of hesitation, Ellie nodded.

Jordan suppressed a sigh.

At least the endgame hadn't changed: Getting Lilah Strickland on the inside. Ellie having conversations with Raphael in a safe controlled environment was as far as this would go.

❧

The next step was a visit to Daniel Deane's compound. The family was skittish about having the police, or any outsider, for that matter, on their premises.

Daniel had come to the station once to answer questions regarding his son, and there had never been enough ties to Raphael's actions to justify a warrant. They still didn't have that warrant, but there was enough reason to have another conversation and see what the family would do about Raphael's impending conviction.

Bethany talked strategy to their small group, making it clear that this wasn't an ordinary interview.

"When you talk to Daniel Deane, make it clear that these are follow-up questions about Raphael. I don't want him to think we might be on to them. Jordan, I want you to take the lead on this, but I'll go with you. A couple of officers. Like I said, low-key."

At this point, Jordan felt like she just couldn't do right by Ellie and keep her out of the line of fire at the same time. She'd take the risk.

"McCarthy and Marshall."

"Sure." Bethany nodded, ignoring Ellie's disappointed look. "Harding, you can go back to your work with Agent Strickland. We'll fill you in on anything you need to know regarding Raphael."

"Will do," Ellie said curtly. "Just a question."

"Go ahead."

"Four people, how is that low-key? Won't they suspect anything?"

"Believe me, between us and them, this is low-key. We'll talk to you later. Let's go."

Outside the room, Jordan hesitated, wondering if she owed Ellie an explanation. Kate McCarthy had been on this case from the beginning. Besides, they couldn't afford this to look like she was doing her girlfriend any favors, right? She might be able to blame this on Bethany.

As they were walking along the hall to the elevator, Bethany said, "Don't worry. She understands chain of command—and I want her to stay with Lilah."

Jordan almost said thank you, but she knew that Bethany liked meddling far too much, so she remained silent instead, pondering the new developments. What had started out as a murder case was part of something bigger—and worse, happening right here under their noses.

The drive was almost an hour, cityscapes and streets giving way to endlessly stretching fields, farms, and roads. Libby Marshall and Kate McCarthy rode in the squad car behind them.

Bethany didn't seem interested in small talk, so Jordan took the time to take stock of the situation, mentally preparing herself for the interview with a man whose lifestyle she despised. Even if Daniel Deane wasn't involved in Jennifer's death, their ideology was enough to make her stomach churn. Men who thought it was their God-given right to control and punish women. Bad always inspired worse.

In the midst of all this she had to make sure Ellie didn't misunderstand a single thing about the current work situation, which included Bethany, and Valerie Esposito.

For Jordan, it meant a regular confrontation with past mistakes made. For Ellie, it didn't have to mean anything. Maybe she needed to make that even clearer.

There were a couple of cars parked on the side of the road, a small group of men halting their conversation, openly watching as they drove past. Some of them carried rifles.

"And so it begins," Bethany commented.

"You've had a lot of dealings with the rest of the family before—personally, I mean?"

"Some. A really pleasant bunch. You'll see."

They changed onto the driveway leading up to the gate, and from here, Jordan could see the vast expanse of land, and the several buildings arranged in a half circle at the center. Daniel Deane had been to the station once after his son was arrested for murder. He claimed to be devastated that his son had tied their family name to a hideous crime. Apparently, he had decided that his involvement stopped there. He hadn't visited Raphael or gone to any of his court dates.

Jordan reminded herself that the premise had changed—but he wasn't supposed to know.

A man in his early thirties, one of the sons, Samuel, greeted them at the door.

"Police?" He frowned when they identified themselves. "Is this about Raphael?"

"Mr. Deane, we'd like to talk to your father. Is he here?"

Samuel shrugged. "He is, but he won't be happy. I thought we cleared everything up already."

Jordan wondered if anyone actually lived in this building. It looked like there were offices rather than living spaces, and for a compound that housed as many people as it did, it was suspiciously quiet around here.

"I'm sorry about that. These are just routine follow-up questions."

"Follow me." Samuel led them through a maze of corridors, given them a first impression of how big this building was. They arrived in a sitting area on the first floor, a den-style room with lots of dark furniture and hunting trophies mounted on the wall.

"Charming," Jordan remarked after he had instructed them to wait and gone to get Daniel.

"I'm relieved to know you're kidding."

"Ladies." They turned to see Daniel Deane standing in the doorway. "This is unfortunate. As you can imagine, we're still grieving over the tragedy that has fallen upon our family."

"Mr. Deane, thank you for seeing us," Jordan said. "We won't be long."

"I hope so. Our lives are humble, but busy."

Yeah, right. Judging from the amount of land and real estate the brothers owned, humble was not the appropriate term. She kept her voice level and polite anyway.

"As we've told your son, those are routine follow-up questions. We are almost ready to close this case."

"Raphael did something unspeakable. What more questions could you possibly have? If you could tell us why, we'd be grateful, because our family has struggled with this."

"I'm aware, and I'm sorry for that. Did Raphael ever bring Jennifer here? We were told they met in Iowa, and lived with your brother Jeremiah for a while, but she was actually from here. She was supposed to come home for her aunt's funeral."

He shook his head. "I can't imagine what that has to do with your case, Detective. Raphael was...a troubled young man. I had hoped he'd come to his senses, but instead he was starting to sever the ties to the family. If one of us brings in a partner, we want to be sure they are accustomed and appreciative of the lives we live. Jennifer was not. We would have sent her away."

"Yet, when she was found, she was wearing the customary clothing for women in your community. Do you think Raphael had access to that, or knew someone who could get it for him?"

"There is no way anyone of us would desecrate them in such a despicable act, so the answer is no. You might not approve of the way we live, Detective, but we're not murderers. The man who committed this crime is not my son anymore. He's a stranger."

"Is that why you never sent him one of your lawyers?" Bethany asked, and for a split-second, they could see the flash of anger on the man's face.

"Not for this. Unfortunately, we need to have them, because the outside world is slow and resistant to understand the good that we do for so many people...but Raphael is guilty. He has confessed to murdering that young woman. He must face the consequences. If you'll excuse me now, I have work to do as I'm sure you have, too."

"Mr. Deane, thank you for talking to us."

"It's no problem. Any way we can help."

Even though it had been a fairly polite conversation, Jordan couldn't help feeling relieved once they were back at their respective cars. She might be exaggerating, but the atmosphere in the house seemed heavy, the Deanes' friendliness a thin disguise. If only her instincts had always been so precise...

Obviously, almost all the men here, if not all, were armed. In this concentration, they probably had enough weapons for a small army. She began to understand what Bethany had meant by saying their presence was low-key.

"Creepy," she remarked. "He wasn't like that in the first interview."

"It's his turf and his people. That makes all the difference. He knows we could never get a search warrant for any of the compounds as it stands now."

"That, and he doesn't seem to give a damn about what happens to Raphael."

"He really doesn't. They have their scapegoat, life goes on. Now we have to convince Raphael that this is the way it is."

"There's no need for Ellie to deliver the bad news to him," Jordan mused, earning an amused glance from Bethany.

"Are we really going to discuss this?"

Jordan sighed. "I guess not. As long as this is on *our* turf..."

"You have my word. Strickland has been waiting for this opportunity for a long time. I don't think she'd appreciate having it taken away by a local cop."

Jordan shook her head, barely suppressing a smile. With Bethany, it was sometimes hard to tell when she meant to make a compliment or an insult. They could work reasonably well together—they should have never been anything else.

Of course, everything was different with Ellie. She'd have to talk to her sometime soon—and let her make her own decisions. Armed with many good intentions, Jordan was ready for the next part of the day, even though it wouldn't be a pleasant one.

Chapter Four

J ennifer Beaumont's mother was equally as unhappy as Daniel Deane had been to see them. Bethany had joined her after McCarthy and Marshall left for the department.

"I thought you had him. What do you think I can help you with?"

"I hoped we could take another look at Jennifer's room," Jordan said. In this house, the atmosphere was heavy too, but for a completely different reason. Mrs. Beaumont had hoped for her daughter to be here for her sister-in-law's funeral—instead, she had to organize another funeral.

"Why? She hasn't lived here in some time. Why are you not taking the place of those people in Iowa apart? You come to me for questions, but I had to read it in the newspaper that Jennifer might have joined some sort of cult."

"Whether she actually joined the group or not is still subject to speculation," Jordan explained. "She lived with them for a while, and yes, members have been questioned."

"What are you trying to find here?"

"She sent you the bracelet, her grandmother's. Was there any other sort of communication that raised red flags with you?"

Jordan was well aware that she was dodging the question. She wasn't entirely clear on what she was trying to find. The book?

It couldn't be that easy, but maybe they could find any hints that tied Jennifer to the Prophets outside her connection with Raphael—that could mean she had intentionally sought them out to expose them, and it would give them a motive. She might have gone with Iowa rather than the local group in order not to raise suspicion. If Jennifer had researched the Prophets of Better Days and approached Raphael with the intent to gather information, there had to be clues somewhere. She had been careful not to leave traces on electronic devices.

"Not that I can think of. Go, take a look if you must, but you know, cops have already been over things in her bedroom."

"Thank you."

"I put a great deal of trust in your hunches," Bethany said when they were standing in Jennifer's old room, "but what *are* you trying to find? Unless somebody screwed up the search."

"Think about it. At the time, nobody knew about the book. We knew that Jennifer had been in Iowa for the last few months, so everyone was looking for clues there, and trying to trace her steps after the flight. If she had been planning this project for a long time, I bet there is a clue somewhere—something that brings us closer to a motive for the Prophets."

"Okay. Where are we looking?"

"I don't know," Jordan said, walking around the girl's room, studying the bookshelves. High school textbooks, novels, nothing that would have caught anyone's attention.

She opened each drawer of the wooden desk, reached inside to see if anything was taped underneath...no such luck.

"I think you were right when you said it would be too easy," Bethany muttered, but she turned to look at another shelf with various knickknack, opened a make-up case.

They looked behind the bed and under, in the wardrobe, shoe boxes, but finally Jordan had to admit that she'd been wrong.

She was about to apologize to Mrs. Beaumont when the woman in question appeared behind her.

"Detective, I don't know if that's important, but the bracelet came in a box...at the time, no one asked me about it because it was months before she..." She swallowed hard. "Before Jennifer died." She handed the small leather-bound jewelry box to Jordan. "Jennifer gave me no explanation as to why she was sending it back, but I always thought that the box wasn't just for protection, but that she meant to tell me she was sorry somehow. I don't know what I'm saying. Maybe it's nothing. I kept it in any case."

"Thank you, Mrs. Beaumont. We'll look into that."

Jordan carefully put the box into an evidence bag. "Thank you so much for your time. And I promise you, we'll let you know if there's anything new."

Bethany drove on the way back, while Jordan regarded the box from all angles.

"What are you thinking? Prints? False bottom?"

"Hopefully, all of the above. Jennifer was resourceful if she managed to do her research, get into the compound and get out, at least for long enough to hide her book somewhere. It's kind of what you are trying to pull off with Strickland."

"Yeah, and something no one has ever done before," Bethany said somberly. "Don't tell anyone I said that, but I really hope we're doing the right thing here. I believe she's ready, but that doesn't mean it's not dangerous."

"At least she knows what she's in for." A moment later, Jordan wasn't too proud of all the implications of her words. In order to stop criminals, they took risks. All of them.

"Yes, she does," Bethany affirmed, not taking the bait. "Let's see if we can get any prints off this and then take it apart. If that doesn't do anything, Ellie can pay another visit to Raphael tomorrow."

Jordan checked the time on her cell phone, realizing she had missed a call from Ellie.

The day had gotten away from her. She wasn't too happy to have spent most of it with her ex, but on the bright side, they were managing polite interaction. It was something.

At the end of the day, Ellie was relieved to escape the office and tons of dusty files and walk outside into the sunshine. She didn't mind the work, thought in fact it was as fascinating as it was infuriating to learn about these men and their delusions of grandeur they had translated into a business...but she'd started to feel a little caged.

She might also feel a bit jealous of Lilah who would go all the way, inside. Ellie knew she had no reason for those senti-ments—after all, she was following her own career. At least, up to the point where Jordan's protective instincts kicked in. No, that wasn't fair either. They had both been through enough to be cautious for themselves, and each other.

All she wanted was to lay the day to rest and maybe have a drink. She called Jordan but got no answer. Next, to decide where to go...After the tragic end of what used to be everyone's favorite hangout, the *Code 7*, many of her colleagues had re-grouped and chosen the *Night Shift*, another bar not far from the precinct, to meet after work. Then again, Bethany might be there, and Valerie Esposito as well.

"Hey. You're waiting for Jordan?" She turned to Kate who had come up behind her.

"Yes...no...I'm not sure. She hasn't called me back, so I guess I won't see her tonight."

Kate waited patiently until Ellie had sorted out her thoughts and decided what she wanted to say.

"No trouble. We've just been busy today. Would you like a drink?"

Kate laughed. "I thought you'd never ask. *Night Shift*?"

"I thought we could go to the *D&T*. It's a couple of blocks farther, but I think their happy hour is still on."

"Happy Hour sounds great to me. I'm in."

They walked in silence for a few minutes while Ellie contemplated that she had little reason to complain. Kate had invested a lot when this was still a missing persons case—now they had gone from a brutal murder to a conspiracy, and probably many more stories.

"What were those people like in real life?" she asked.

Kate shrugged. "Surprisingly polite, though they made sure we knew they all had guns. We only saw men the whole time. There's something creepy about them for sure."

"I don't think I ever said that, but I'm really sorry about Jennifer."

"Yeah, I know. Thank you. We were all hoping to find her alive, but that's not how it always works out." She let out a frustrated sigh. "Sometimes I feel like we are hardly making a difference, or only after the fact, trying to patch things up."

Ellie had felt that way before, but she had also promised herself to reach beyond her own frustration, anger, and fear.

"We have a chance to bring them all down. That will make a difference to many," she said.

"Let's hope. So, what's new with you? You spent all day with the agent?"

They had reached the front door of the *D&T* and walked inside.

"She's cool," Ellie admitted. "Very ambitious."

"Like someone I know."

"I hope you mean that in a nice way."

"How else would I mean it? Come on, I know you have plans. I'm glad you're going for it. Detective Harding. It has a nice ring to it."

That, Ellie couldn't deny. "I agree. Let's drink to that."

Checking her cell phone, she saw that Jordan had texted her. *Sorry I couldn't make it. See you tomorrow night.* All right then. They had made big steps, even lived together for a while, taken a vacation together—one day apart wasn't a big deal, even if Jordan spent that day working with Bethany.

⁂

No problem, have a good night, Ellie had sent with a heart emoji. Jordan was still sitting at her desk, fairly annoyed with herself as she stared at the parts of the leather-bound box. There had been prints, but so far, nothing conclusive. No hidden compartments. Nothing.

She believed that Jennifer Beaumont had chosen her steps carefully—if the tell-all book existed as Raphael Deane claimed, she had to have known they were dangerous. She would hide it in a safe place. Just like the mother, Jordan was sure that sending the bracelet was of relevance, but was it really connected to the book? Excitement had gotten the better of her, and she'd imagined she'd find a key or a note getting them closer to where those writings might be.

Bethany was right—they needed this, but they needed much more than that to prove that the Prophets were implicated in Jennifer Beaumont's murder.

They needed Lilah to succeed.

"Still trying to solve the puzzle?" Derek said when he stopped by her desk.

Jordan answered with a frustrated shrug. "I'm beginning to think I got it all wrong. Why couldn't she just hide the key to a safe deposit box in there?"

"Too easy," he said good-naturedly.

"Yeah, I heard that one before."

"Would you like to come over for a beer?"

Since Derek was dating Kate, and Ellie was living with Kate, they spent a lot more time together off duty than before.

"Thanks, but not tonight. I'm going to head home."

"All right. See you tomorrow."

The half hour drive to her neighborhood went a long way to clear her mind. While it might be unpractical in the morning to live that far away from her job, she benefited from the distance once the workday was over. Then again, she had spent most nights of the past month at Ellie's, and on the weekends, Ellie usually stayed over…This was a situation still in limbo, but it would be tough to change.

Jordan prepared a frozen meal in the microwave and opened the last beer in the fridge, carrying all of it to the small deck behind the house. Would they ever solve this? She liked living here, the peace and quiet after a day in the city. She hardly ever heard or saw the neighbors, except when they were coincidentally getting the mail or taking out the garbage at the same time.

She lived here regardless of the fact that her realtor had turned out to be a serial killer who had been targeting her…In Jordan's opinion, this was part of her revenge, having a home and a life with the woman she loved, regardless. Only Ellie had no intention of moving here.

Perhaps they could work out a compromise, eventually find something that was closer to the city center but still offered some peace and quiet. Maybe at some point, keeping this house would no longer serve her, just like the anger towards her birth-parents had lost some of its function.

She had met with Kathryn and heard her explanations once. It hadn't dramatically changed their relationship or Jordan's childhood memories. If she was going to see her another time, it wasn't because there was any way to justify Kathryn and Jim's actions—but she wanted to live in the present. In moving forward, with her life in general and Ellie in particular, she had to clear up everything that had stood in her way for so long, first.

Jordan considered calling Ellie again, then decided it was too late. She scrolled through her address book and found Kathryn's number.

"Hey. I was wondering if you'd like to meet for lunch this Friday," she typed, hesitating for the span of a few seconds, before she sent it. A couple of minutes later, she felt foolish. Then the phone rang.

"Hi."

"Hello, Jordan."

There was a moment of silence, surprise maybe, whatever the reason for the awkward pause, Jordan already regretted approaching her. What had she expected?

"I would love to see you," Kathryn said. "Thank you."

"Okay, great. There's a diner a block from the precinct, *Suzie's*? I'll meet you there." She ended the call before either of them had a chance to change their mind.

⁂

The next morning, Ellie was called straight to the conference room. Jordan was already there, with Bethany and Lilah Strickland.

"All right," Bethany began. "We know that Daddy is not going to send any lawyers, and neither will any of the uncles. Ellie, I want you to communicate this clearly to Raphael: He's on his own. The book angle is still a good one, but it hasn't gotten us far yet. I don't want you to do your best. I want you to do better."

No pressure.

Ellie was far past being intimidated by her. She wanted to get the job done, and she appreciated every moment she got to learn from more experienced colleagues, especially women. It was nevertheless an awkward situation, all of them on the same case, Lilah, of course, being oblivious. There was always a bigger picture to consider.

"Will do. Did you ask any of them if they knew about the book? Daniel, or the others?"

"Not yet. We don't want to tip them off, let them know we are aware of it," Jordan explained.

"Okay, I understand. Let's do this."

Ellie wasn't scared to be in the same room with Raphael Deane, though his sickening attitude did make it seem smaller and more claustrophobic. Nevertheless, she plastered a smile on her face before she walked inside.

"Hey, Raphael."

He looked surprised. "I didn't think you were going to come back. Didn't anyone around here tell you what I did?"

She sat across from him. "I know what you did, but you asked me to check something for you, and I did. I'm afraid I have bad news for you."

"What do you mean?"

"My colleagues talked to your father. He confirmed that the family is not going to pay for legal representation."

"You're lying!" he yelled, startling her.

Ellie flinched, but she remained seated, waiting for him to take a deep breath and calm down. He shook his head. "No. You're just trying to trick me into something."

"Yes, because that has worked so well for us, hasn't it? Look, you really think I'd be wasting my time telling you this if it wasn't true? I have a job to do. The reason I'm here is that you're a friend of Rhonda's. If there's something you need to talk about with your public defender, you better do it soon."

"They don't understand," he claimed.

"That's perhaps true. I admit I don't understand it either. If Jennifer was telling lies in her book, you could have sued her, get more money than she'd ever make with it. Doesn't that make more sense than killing her?"

"The damage would have been done. I'm sorry if that's not what you want to hear. Why don't you go back to your job? You can't help me."

Ellie pushed her chair back and got up. "Maybe you're right. I can't do anything for you unless you cut the bullshit and start talking to me. If we found that book, it would be much easier to argue that you panicked, being already under so much pressure from your family. If they find it first...well, let's say you're running out of options fast. I'm not going to come back."

Her heart was pounding as she walked to the door, hoping she hadn't laid it on too thick.

She couldn't hesitate too much either, or he would call her bluff.

At the last moment, he said, "Please, wait."

Ellie turned around, leaning against the door.

"Why? You made it clear that you're not going to work with me. You want to take all the blame, that's fine with me. I can tell Rhonda that."

"You don't understand. If I do this, I won't be safe. Neither of us is ever going to be safe again."

Those words gave her a chill, but she took a couple of steps towards him.

"They are not almighty, but they have harmed many people. You can help us put a stop to that, and we can help you. That is not a trick or a lie. You murdered somebody, and you will be held accountable, but the ones who put you up to that should be too."

"What do you want?" he asked, his tone resigned. "You said it yourself, they're not going to listen to me on anything now."

"That's right." Ellie sat back down. "But you grew up with them, lived with them for most of your life. Tell me how we get in."

He shook his head. "You can't just knock on the door and asked to be let in. They will smell a cop."

How original, she thought. "So, what do we do?"

"I'm not sure."

Ellie got to her feet. "Right."

"I'm not sure if it's going to work, all right? There's a bar a few miles out, where the guys go. Over the years, they've brought back a girl or two. You know, the kind you wouldn't miss right away."

Listening, Ellie had to swallow her anger once more. She had to remind herself that if she could see this through, it would only help the greater good, and her career in the process—valid reasons not to show how much he disgusted her.

"Come on, don't think I'm stupid. I've seen their websites. They consider themselves holy men, chosen...and you're telling me they go to a seedy bar to hook up and bring back some lost sheep?"

"Believe it or not." He shrugged. "At home, everyone plays by the rules. My dad and uncles wouldn't like it if they knew—they think they go and observe, then approach someone if they fit the requirement. What do they expect?" he said with a cruel laugh. "With the robot wives they have at home? A man needs some kind of outlet."

After he had given her the address, Ellie was more than happy to leave the room.

"Brilliant," Bethany commented. "Purity of body and mind, that's what the manifesto says, huh? I guess some of the boys didn't get that memo. "I will let you go back to your day job now while Agent Strickland and I work on further preparations. We might need you for backup later, or sometime this week."

"That's it?" After spending another couple of hours with Deane, this moment felt rather anti-climactic to Ellie.

"Well, yeah, unless you'd like to join me and Lilah for lunch."

"I think she's got plans already," Jordan said with a hint of amusement. "Ellie?"

"Yeah, sure."

Truth be told, Ellie would have liked to go home and have a long shower, but that wasn't an option right now. Lunch with Jordan was a preferable alternative.

"Wow, that was fast," she said when they were on the way to Jordan's car. "I didn't think they would shut us out so early."

"Get used to it. This is not even shutting out. They're going to need some of us when they set up the specifics."

"Okay. How was your evening?"

"I had to get over not finding the magic key...I think I did. You did great, finding out about the book, and getting him to cooperate."

After everything they'd been through together, Ellie still felt a little flustered at the compliment. They had arrived at the restaurant, and Jordan held the door open for her.

"Thank you," she said, meaning the gesture and so much more. "I think he was at this point where he really wanted to talk. I hope he's not feeding us a load of crap."

"Strickland is well prepared. She'll be careful," Jordan offered as they sat down at a table in the corner. "Look...I'm really sorry about all of this."

"It's okay. I heard you, I swear. About everything."

She wasn't going to obsess about Esposito any longer, or any assignment she might have gotten out of this case. She, they both had to move forward.

They were silent for a few moments, before Jordan said, "I called Kathryn. I'm going to see her for lunch on Friday."

It was a bit of a surprise that she had contacted her so soon.

"That's a good thing, right?"

"I suppose. I don't want to give them so much power over what I think or feel anymore. They have to live their lives. I have to live mine. And speaking of which, would you mind if I stayed over tonight? As long as we're in limbo with this case, I'd like to get some work done and maybe take Friday afternoon off. We could make it a long weekend?" Jordan asked, sounding hopeful.

"I'd love that." There had hardly been any off time since their vacation. "As long as you don't mind that I take a bit of time to study."

"It's getting serious now."

Jordan's proud smile was another affirmation that she was on the right track, after getting praise from Bethany of all people. In the past year, Ellie had kept as close to detective work as her job allowed, and it was finally paying off.

"No kidding. I can't believe it's almost here. I decided to do this during the first weeks on the job."

"And you might be able to move upstairs right away. Rumor has it Waters is retiring at the end of the year—but don't tell anyone yet."

This was exciting news, her long-held plans about to come true. She and Jordan already worked well together. Ellie hoped that would continue once they did it more often.

"Would you really be okay, working this closely all the time?"

Jordan smiled ruefully. "I will be. Don't worry. I heard you too. I have to stop freaking out every time you have a tough assignment. I get it. Sometimes, it's just...hard."

"I understand. On the bright side...We have the rest of our lives to get used to it, right?" Ellie was well aware that she might be getting ahead of herself, but she was confident, and Jordan needed that little push every once in a while.

"We do."

Chapter Five

J ordan had, as she'd told Ellie, caught up on her paperwork,
but her thoughts kept wandering back to that small box.
There was a name engraved, the manufacturer, but the letters
were mostly unreadable. A serial number on the bottom—it
looked as if it had been handwritten. None of this was of
any help, and the only fingerprints belonged to Jennifer Beaumont. Her mother had said that the bracelet wasn't worth that
much—why had Jennifer chosen this particular box to send it?
Maybe it meant nothing, and she was grasping at straws.

What if it did?

She went back to studying the files on the Prophets of Better
Days, notes from Ellie and Lilah Strickland. There were certain
behavioral patterns one could deduce from their online presence, but they were careful not to go beyond a certain point.
All of it, promoting a woman's role in the home, lamenting the
"homosexual agenda" and lack of morals in society, it wasn't
new or original. There was no way of holding them accountable
for spreading prejudice and harmful stereotypes—but Bethany
and her colleagues believed they had done more than that.

The book would help a great deal. Raphael Deane claimed
that Jennifer Beaumont had never told him where she'd hidden
it. Again, she studied the different parts of the box. It was simply
made, wood and velvet fabric, leather on the outside. What if

the clue was in the box, not the bracelet? She went back to the files where the business side of the Prophets was detailed: Farming was mostly for self-sustenance, but they sold a handful of products.

Leather? She found the website of a small company offering leather-binding for books and knickknacks. It was owned by one of Daniel's nephews, Nathan, who lived on the local compound. He was Jeremiah's son and had moved here from the Iowa compound.

She picked up the phone to call Bethany. Jordan assumed that while Nathan was listed as the owner of the company, the women would do a lot of the work. This could be a chance for Lilah to make some friends on the inside.

"That's a good idea," Bethany said. "Is Harding anywhere near? Don't make plans for tonight."

⁂

Lilah Strickland had a complete story and persona, and she would try to catch the attention of some family members. Raphael Deane had given them the address of a local pub where some of the male family members could be found on any given night, looking for an adventure or a soul to save, sometimes both. He'd told them that "they can't resist a good story."

Aside from the women born into their group and living on the compounds for the majority of their lives, they looked for recruits every once in a while, but the process was complicated. If someone came to them, they'd be suspicious, paranoid.

If Strickland managed to present herself as somebody who needed saving in their opinion, inspiring them to take action—there was a good chance. This was what they suspected had happened to Jennifer. This was what almost happened to Rhonda.

Jordan was disgusted that something like this could go on close to her hometown. She didn't want Ellie anywhere near it. She didn't want to be anywhere near it, but under the circumstances, neither of them had a choice.

For some reason, Bethany seemed eager to advance Ellie's career. She might still be trying to make amends. There was no reason to suspect ulterior motives. Jordan found it odd, nonetheless.

We had a deal. Jordan didn't say it out loud, even though she strongly disagreed with Bethany's assessment of the situation. The problem was, she couldn't voice her concern without sounding like everything she'd told Ellie over lunch was just lip service.

"So Strickland will hang out there every night until one of them tries to pick her up?"

"Start conversations first," Bethany said, and Agent Russo nodded. "We'll be listening in, getting a feel for how they react to her."

Raphael had also assured them that there were certain trigger words that would guarantee the family's interest. Abortion. Lesbian. A pregnancy out of wedlock—anything that would trigger their self-righteous anger about the conduct of women.

Neither Jordan nor Bethany could go in because Daniel Deane knew them, but Agent Russo would be watching Strickland. For some reason, Bethany thought it would help if Ellie was there too. That was different from talks with Raphael in a controlled environment. The set-up was supposed to put Strickland on their radar, but the same could potentially happen to Ellie.

She, however, didn't seem much concerned about it.

"Sure, I can blend in," she said. "Sell the story if someone wants to hear it."

Jordan caught Bethany's quick sideways glance on her.

"Be careful," Bethany said. "Do it if you have the opportunity, but don't lay it on too thick. Remember, Lilah's the star here."

"Understood."

"Everybody knows what they're supposed to do, great. Let's have a girls' night out."

Much to his credit, Russo didn't comment on that, and he didn't even make a face. Everyone was too focused on this opportunity that might not come back.

The Prophets might be cautious so soon after Jennifer's murder, but Lilah's would be a story they wouldn't be able to resist. That's what they all hoped.

ೋ

Ellie had always been observant, but since the incident that made the *Code 7* go up in flames, she paid even more attention to the audience when going to a new place. She already knew that she wouldn't find any women who lived with the cult, here. The men left the compound more often, Raphael had said, for business and pleasure purposes. The wives remained oblivious in all of it—or at least, they were supposed to be.

Too much curiosity was usually followed by swift punishment, a lesson taught to all children on the compound. She still despised Raphael Deane for what he had done—it wasn't hard to put the pieces together though, the environment that had made him think he needed to call out Rhonda on her clothing choices and keep Jennifer from revealing the secrets at all costs.

She could easily understand what had Jordan on edge. They'd had their share of dealing with megalomaniac male criminals. The structure of the Prophets' family and other groups like that made it much harder to get to them and prove they were actually committing crimes according to the letter of the law. It shouldn't be so hard to dismantle a women-hating cult.

She took a seat at a table from where she had a good vantage point for the whole bar. A staircase led to a small gallery, and on the main floor, about twenty tables were strewn across the space, the bar spanning the far wall. Russo was sitting at another table, Lilah at the bar. Ellie scanned the room, unobtrusively studying the men present. There was a group of four people, two men, two women—judging from their body language and clothing, they weren't what Raphael had described. A couple of women sat at a small table by the window on the other side, and three tables were occupied by men. One of them had a sparsely clad woman sitting perching on his lap. So much for morals. Their clothing was simple, and, if you looked closely, almost like a uniform.

Ellie got up and went to the bar to order a beer, steering close enough to their table that she could hear the woman laugh. She seemed a little blitzed, but not in distress. Ellie assumed that she would be safe for the night—she was probably not the type these men deemed worth saving, and they didn't want to draw too much attention to them either.

She caught Russo's stern glance and resisted the urge to give him a shrug. She couldn't spend the whole night wondering about this woman...and maybe there was even a chance to talk to her...

Ellie ordered her beer, and while she was waiting, saw one of the men from the table get up and walk over to where Lilah sat on a barstool, nursing her Coke. She was looking pensive and sad. According to her undercover story, she had reason to be. "Lilly" had been kicked out of her home when pregnant as a teenager. She had given the baby up for adoption, had to live in her car for a while and was now working three jobs to keep a roof over her head. She was looking for guidance, but unable to find it. She was scared of the future, blaming herself for the events that had led her to this place.

If asked, Ellie was someone who knew her, not well, but from what she'd heard Lilly needed to get her life together. She would do anything for it. She needed to come home.

Assured that Lilah was making first contact as planned, and that Raphael had obviously not lied to them, Ellie directed her attention back to the other woman. At second glance, she was more intoxicated than Ellie had thought, or maybe the woman had continued to drink really fast in the few minutes it took her to order the beer and go back to her place.

Ellie sat back and continued to watch her. The entitlement and exploitation of women by the brothers and their sons was outrageous. They expected their wives to cater to every one of their demands, punished them if they didn't, and they cheated on them, picking up women in bars. Each compound had a schoolhouse, but it was clear that the children also had to do a great deal of work on the farms and in the other businesses.

Meanwhile, Lilah seemed in deep conversation with the man who had taken a seat beside her.

Nobody was approaching Ellie. Jordan would be more than happy with that.

The other woman got to her feet. She seemed unsteady as she walked to the stairs that led down to the restrooms. The man on whose lap she'd been sitting got up a moment later, laughing with his friends before he followed her. Ellie cast another glance at Lilah Strickland who seemed to be doing just fine, and got up as well, walking across the room and down the stairs. The couple was standing in front of the door to the Ladies' room, kissing, but it didn't take her long to hear faint protest from the woman. She could barely hold herself up, let alone push him back.

"Hey, are you okay?"

"She's fine," the man answered for her. "Mind your own business."

"I would, if you didn't block the door."

Grudgingly, he stepped aside. "Now get lost. Nothing to see here."

Ellie knew all to well that she needed to be careful, not to blow Lilah's cover, Russo's, and her own—but there was no way she'd let her alone with him.

"Oh, I think your friend needs to touch up her make-up, right? Why don't you come with me for a moment?"

She could tell by the relief clearly showing on the woman's face that she was on the right path. The man, however, wasn't so accommodating.

"Bitch, get lost!" He pushed her, finding himself facing the wall up close the next moment. "Are you crazy?"

"Now let her do her make-up in peace, all right? You don't want any trouble. Neither do I. You," she addressed the woman, "is there someone you can call?"

A timid shake of the head was the answer. "It's okay. We'll find someone." She let go of the man, taking a step back. "Why don't you get lost?"

To her surprise, he spun around and headed back up the stairs. Ellie's charge stumbled into the bathroom and sank back against the wall, sliding to the floor.

"Thank you," she murmured.

"You're welcome," Ellie said as she closed the door. "Please, don't pass out. What's your name?"

"Fiona."

"Fiona. Good. I'll make sure you get home safely. Give me a moment, okay?"

Ellie scrolled through the numbers in her phone. Obviously, she could call neither Kate nor Libby—both of them had accompanied Jordan and Bethany to Daniel Deane's. After a moment of hesitation, she hit Derek Henderson's number, hoping he would be inclined to do her a favor.

"Ellie," he said, surprised. "Aren't you working with Jordan and Dr. Roberts right now?"

"Yes. Sort of. Well, not sort of, but there's a small problem. I'm here in the Ladies' room with a woman who's almost passed out, and I need someone to drive her home. Obviously, I can't do it myself or ask any of the other cops here. Kate was with Jordan when they went to see Deane, so I was hoping you could..."

"No problem. Just give me directions."

"Wow, thanks. I owe you."

"That's okay. Think of it as paying for coffee, beer, and hot water."

"That works. Thank you." Ellie described the way to the bar, fairly amused at his reference to the odd arrangement the four of them had. The truth was it was practical for everyone. Jordan might grumble about it from time to time, but she didn't really mind. Both Kate and Derek were easygoing and uncomplicated. For the time being, this was the best solution.

After ending the call, she turned back to Fiona, crouched in front of her and shook her slightly.

"Hey. Can you stand up?"

"I want to sleep," Fiona muttered.

"Soon, I promise. Can you tell me where you live?"

"I don't feel so good."

"Oh no. Not now."

"I'm sorry. Sorry."

When Fiona leaned forward and threw up, Ellie all but jumped back, fortunately in time. She grabbed a few paper towels from the dispenser and handed them to Fiona who cleaned herself up with shaking hands. In her purse, Ellie found a pack of gum.

"All right. We should get you out of here. My colleague will be here soon."

She didn't get much of a reaction from the distraught woman.

About twenty minutes later, there was a knock on the door. Fiona jumped.

"Don't worry," Ellie told her and opened the door to Derek who cast a quick glance at her companion.

"I don't think Dr. Roberts will be happy about all this."

"Everything else is going as planned." Ellie shrugged. "I'll go back in there in a moment, but I wanted to make sure she's okay. This is Fiona. One of the guys upstairs got a little too hands-on."

"I feel funny," Fiona said miserably. "This is strange. I only had one beer. Just one, I swear."

Ellie exchanged a look with Derek, assuming he was thinking the same.

"Fiona, maybe we should stop by the hospital," he said.

"She said I could go home and sleep. Who are you anyway?"

"He's a cop," Ellie said. "I need to stay here, but please, go with him. You'll be safe."

She waited until both of them were out of her sight, then another moment before she made her way back up. Lilah was sitting alone at the bar. The table where Fiona had sat with the group of men was empty, but a few newcomers had arrived.

It didn't take long for one of them to pass by her table where her untouched beer was warm by now.

"Hey, baby…You're not here all by yourself?"

From the looks of his clothes, he was part of the Prophets of Better Days family.

"I'm waiting for my boyfriend," Ellie said.

"Let me know if he doesn't show up. I can give you a ride home."

"Oh, I'm pretty sure that he will show up, but thanks."

"No problem. Please, don't be shy to ask. It's not safe for women to be out alone. I guess you heard about the one that got murdered."

"I did, but now you really got me worried about getting in a car with anyone..."

He laughed. "You don't have to. I am married, but we take care of our neighbors. I am Seth."

"Nice to meet you. Ellie."

"It's nice to meet you too. Can I?" He didn't wait for an answer but pulled himself a chair.

"Sure. What do you mean, you take care of your neighbors?"

"We try to educate. Look, someone like her..." He nodded towards Lilah. "She's a beautiful girl, don't you think? Why does she have to draw attention to herself, being dressed like that?"

For a moment, Ellie was speechless.

"Well, I'd think that is her business. I hear she's had a tough time, so maybe she just wants to enjoy a night out."

"But what if something happens to her, and then all of a sudden, it's everybody's business?"

"What can you do?"

"Talk to her, help her understand? In any case, it never harms to monitor the situation."

As in stalking. This was certainly informative. "You come here often? To make sure everyone's all right?"

"Every once in a while."

"Well, it's good to know we can hang out here safely, but you might be right. My boyfriend's not going to come—I'll call a cab."

"Thanks for the conversation."

"You're welcome," Ellie said and got up. "Maybe you can help her. She could use some...guidance."

His gaze was on Lilah/Lilly when she left the bar. Ellie wondered if Derek had gotten any helpful information from Fiona.

Chapter Six

S pending the evening with her ex in a non-descript van, spying on people hitting on each other, wasn't Jordan's first choice for a Friday evening. On the bright side, the space didn't feel nearly as claustrophobic as she'd feared. This was about the job and nothing else.

Agent Strickland couldn't appear too easy, so she started a conversation with the first guy, but didn't push too hard on the seeking-guidance story. He didn't say anything incriminating. The second one did.

Jordan acknowledged with a wry smile when Bethany groaned in frustration.

"And this is why we can't have nice things. Who does this guy think he is?"

She couldn't agree more. This one was beyond annoying, starting out with dubious compliments, then rapidly heading down the slippery slope to full-on insults.

"Hey, what's it to you how I dress?" Lilah said. She was good, a hundred percent in character. The star of the show.

"Well, I can't not see it, can I? You do it on purpose. Do you have a price?"

"Here we go," Jordan said, shaking her head.

"What do you mean?"

"Come on, you know what I mean."

The conversation continued in that vein, nothing surprising yet. The surprise was when Derek's car pulled up in front of the bar.

Bethany frowned. "What is he doing here?"

"Don't look at me, I have no idea."

"This better not be work. Lilah is doing well. I don't want any of the locals screwing this up."

"Easy. There's a local sitting right next to you."

"I'm not talking about you," Bethany muttered.

"For all we know, he's just going to have a beer."

"Right. And for that, he had to come here of all places."

Jordan had to admit that her partner's appearance in this place was odd. She doubted he even knew they were here tonight. And hadn't he been talking about going out with McCarthy tonight? The story became even stranger when a few minutes after, he returned with a woman by his side who could barely walk upright. Jordan cringed at the image. He'd once come to pick her up after a drunken binge, but at least, she'd made it home without incident.

"I wonder if his girlfriend knows about this," Bethany remarked.

"Let's not jump to conclusions, all right?"

They returned to listening to the conversation Lilah and her acquaintance were having.

The tone had changed again, becoming more conversational, friendlier as Lilah pretended to see reason in the man's out of line behavior.

"I'm sorry, you misunderstood," she said. "I've really had a bad time. Sometimes it feels like no one cares—and no one would mind if I was gone."

"Then you need to change who you're with, find people who respect you for who you are."

"Sounds great. I'm not sure that species actually exists."

"You'd be surprised."

"That means you know better people, or are you just really hopeful?"

"I never lose hope in people's ability to change," he said proudly. "Lilly, can I see you again?"

A pause. "Maybe."

"I'll be here tomorrow. Will you?"

"I might. I enjoyed talking to you, but I need to go home. I have to work tomorrow."

"Come back and we'll talk some more."

Jordan pressed Derek's number on her cell phone, surprised when he answered right away.

"I know what you're going to ask me, but we have a bit of a situation here," he said.

"Where are you?"

"At the hospital with a woman named Fiona Grayson. It appears that she has been drugged."

"The woman from the bar? How did you know?"

"Ellie called me."

"Oh."

"That's all you have to say? She handled the situation pretty well, getting Grayson out without raising anyone's suspicion."

"No, it's great she did that. Look, we're busy here, you catch me up later?"

"Sure."

Jordan ended the call, wondering whether Bethany would share Derek's assessment of the situation.

They met back at the station where Lilah was first to report, then Russo stated his observations. Apparently, Raphael had told the truth. Some of the male cult members frequented the place to meet women, to berate them and hook up with them equally. They were looking for the vulnerable ones.

BARBARA WINKES

"So far, lots of bad manners, no crimes though he wants to see me again. Maybe I'll be introduced to the family," Lilah concluded.

"Excuse me, no crime?" Ellie said incredulously.

"Yeah, about that." Bethany crossed her arms across her chest. "You had clear instructions. Eyes on Lilah at all times, pushing her story if the occasion arises. Don't, and I think I told you that a couple of times, don't draw attention to yourself."

"What was I supposed to do? He was feeling her up in the hallway, against her will, and now we know she was drugged! We can quickly follow up on this. Both Fiona and I can identify him."

Bethany looked frustrated, and Jordan could easily guess why. If the Prophets got tipped off about the police presence in their favorite hangout, they might not come out again. However, she couldn't tell them not to follow up on a crime.

"You do that but be careful. It would be easy to screw this up right now and lose the only chance we have."

"It fits the pattern," Ellie insisted. "This is exactly how they treat women, and you wanted proof that they use more than words. You're welcome."

Jordan hid a smile, secretly thrilled that Ellie was standing her ground. She might be treading a line though, judging from Bethany's expression.

"Do your job. Don't ever get cocky. It could get you killed, or someone you care about."

Ellie held her head up.

"I'm aware. So, do we bring him in for questioning?"

"Not you. That could compromise Lilah's cover."

"Speaking of which, I almost forgot—the guy who was talking to me, Seth? He gave me his number and offered me a ride. He also told me he was married. It's like they can't control themselves the moment they see a single woman."

"Okay, guys, same time tomorrow," Bethany said, effectively dismissing Ellie. She hadn't forgotten about her though. "You don't need to come, Harding. It's too much of a risk. Talk to Raphael about this Seth guy. Other than that, don't draw any more attention to yourself."

"But..."

"That's all. Have a good night."

Jordan had predicted Ellie would not be happy with this outcome. She'd been right.

"What is wrong with her?" she exclaimed once they were in Jordan's car. "I did nothing wrong. In fact, I prevented a crime from happening, and I did it without jeopardizing the operation. Does she want me to help or not?"

"It's not personal."

Ellie snorted.

"I swear. She's up for a promotion, so she has to consider every step very carefully."

"Again. I didn't do anything wrong."

"I agree. Once we start to pick up people, things could get messy though. Strickland needs to create more of a rapport. She's doing okay, but I think you got more out of Seth."

"So we wait until one of them actually goes through with an assault? We—" She broke off her sentence as she'd probably come to the same chilling conclusion Jordan had. It might have already happened.

"We don't wait, but we have to be careful," Jordan said. "With all the things they suspect going on inside...those people are pretty nuts already, and it will be worse if they feel cornered."

"Yeah, I know." Ellie sighed. "It's only been a few days, and already...dealing with this stuff, it's icky. I mean we know that kind of attitude exists, but concentrated like that..."

"I know what you mean. Makes you want to take a long hot shower to wash it off."

Jordan was aware of Ellie's quick sideways glance, indicating she knew that Jordan's mind had briefly wandered to a place that had nothing to do with the Prophets of Better Days. "It's late," she said, trying to make the conversation a little lighter again. "So maybe in order to save time, you'd like to take that shower with me?"

Ellie smiled gratefully. "That's a great idea. Especially since we never know how long the hot water will last."

"That's a reason."

"Yeah, but I have many more."

The apartment was dark and silent when they came home. In all likelihood, they would have the place to themselves for a while, if not for the whole night. It didn't take long for the bathroom floor to be littered with clothes. Ellie leaned back against the cold tile, closing her eyes as the hot water came rushing down, giving over her body to Jordan's warm confident touch, her hands slick with the peach-scented shower gel, washing away the last bit of tension and frustration. Eventually, their mission went from comforting to exciting, and Ellie followed easily. She shivered with the pleasant sensations, each brush of fingertips, each movement bringing her closer to the edge. Jordan kissed her deeply and urgently when her body was ready for the free fall, pulling her closer. For several moments, all she could do was try to stay upright and breathe.

Ellie wasn't yet ready to have a conversation in which she'd have to admit that Bethany made the right call. In fact, she didn't want to talk about Bethany at all.

There was no time to waste, especially considering that they could run out of hot water sometime soon. She went to her knees, enjoying the feel of Jordan's fingers tangling in her hair as she struggled to anchor herself.

They were together, and they were okay, no matter what personal or professional challenges might wait. The water raining down on them started to turn tepid, and then cold, but only moments away from her goal, Ellie didn't give up. She wasn't a quitter.

Shivering and laughing, they got out of the shower a couple of minutes later.

Kate returned by the time they had put on robes and prepared a late-night snack.

"What a day," she said. Neither Ellie nor Jordan had anything to argue.

As much as Jordan loved the peace and quiet of her neighborhood, she loved waking up with Ellie next to her, Ellie kissing her awake more. She knew Ellie got immensely frustrated with detours and roadblocks, whether supervisors or criminals put them in her way. They didn't exactly have the same coping strategies when it came to the darker moments of their lives, but Jordan could work with Ellie's. Perfectly. Their timing was impeccable too.

She was still gasping for breath when they heard the shower being turned off. Ellie wore a smug smile, and she had reason to.

"Got that out of your system? I'm glad I could help."

Ellie picked up a shirt and shorts and put them on. "Oh, there's nothing I need to get out of my system, but this is the best start of the day. I'll lay low until I pass my test...I didn't even expect Bethany to cut me as much slack as she did. I can't wait to finish up for the week so we can get out of town."

"Me too." If the past few hours were any indication, the weekend could only be amazing. The only thing putting a damper on Jordan's excellent mood was when she remembered the date she'd made for tomorrow's lunch.

"Kathryn is coming to your house again?"

Ellie was good at reading her. To Jordan's surprise, it didn't spook her—then again, Ellie knew not to poke and prod.

"No, I suggested a restaurant. I think we're at that stage where we can behave in public, no yelling, no blackmailing."

"That's good. It can only get better from here, right?"

"Let's hope." Jordan wrapped the sheet around her and went in search for her own clothes.

"Want to share the shower again?"

Ellie laughed. "Neither of us is ever going to get to work."

"True. All right, let's hope that it will be Friday afternoon soon. I'll pick you up?"

"I can't wait. Now get in the shower before I change my mind."

***

When Jordan returned, breakfast was ready, and she found Kate and Ellie talking about the previous night's events.

"I hope you don't mind I ruined your evening," Ellie said. "Derek was the only one I could think of at that moment."

"We weren't going to hang out long anyway. Derek was going to see one of his informants."

"Really." It occurred to Jordan that with Bethany in town and Raphael Deane's case pending, she hadn't talked to Derek often lately.

"He didn't say much about it, but the guy didn't show up, and then Ellie called."

"Yeah." Ellie sighed. "I can't help thinking that's the reason why Bethany wants me off the case."

"Does it matter?" Jordan asked softly, and Ellie understood exactly what she meant. She had taken a risk, and for the woman in the bar, it had definitely paid off.

"No, not really. Maybe Derek knows more about how Fiona Grayson is doing. I'm going to ask him."

Ellie would be fine, Jordan reflected. The study material was already piling up in her room, and if Jordan wasn't mistaken, she had been muttering a test answer in her sleep. It was odd to think that she and Bethany actually had a lot in common, intelligence, focus. The difference was, Ellie understood her. Jordan and Bethany had spent almost a decade trying to get each other and failed.

With this clarity, it was a lot easier to put personal issues aside and get the work done, though Jordan doubted she'd be on the case much longer. Once Strickland was on the inside, it would be completely in the hands of the FBI, and locals would be involved if logistics required it, no sooner.

"I need to go," she said. "Come by for lunch if you have the time? It's Doss's birthday. She has a sweet tooth."

"Sounds good. I'll see if I can make it. Speaking of which, have you heard from Darla lately?"

"Not in a while," Jordan said. "She was doing okay the last time she called."

The young woman had been her CI for a couple of years before she decided to make some radical changes in the aftermath of a case that almost turned fatal. Darla had given birth to a baby boy not long ago and seemed to be juggling the different aspects of her life successfully.

Jordan made a mental note to check in on her soon.

"So, things seem to be looking up," Kate remarked when she emptied the last of the coffee pot into Ellie's cup. "You've been working things out?"

The question was completely innocent. There was no reason to blush, but she did anyway.

"It's been good," she said. "Esposito should be the last ex to show up without warning."

Kate laughed. "Rhonda asked you out for a coffee."

"Um, not the same. She's still somewhat related to the case, and of course I didn't go. Now is so much better." She tugged on a strand of her hair, back to her natural color.

"No more compromises, huh? Sounds good to me."

In fact, it was better than good. There had been a few obstacles in their way, but the truth was, Ellie loved her life at this moment. There was one compromise left that on occasion made her uneasy, because she wasn't sure how to approach it with Jordan.

"It is. Well, except maybe for the serial killer house."

"Don't call it that—you're going to freak yourself out." Kate made a face. "You're going to freak me out. He never actually killed anyone in that house, right?"

"That's right, but he still sold it to her. It will always be connected in a way."

"But it's important to Jordan."

"Yes." Ellie drew a deep breath. "I'm sure we'll figure it out. Hey, we have a few minutes left—how about we take a look at the state of *your* relationship?" she asked, making her friend laugh.

"I see. It's going fine. The gossip has pretty much died down—bad metaphor, I know. Still makes me flinch, and how weird is that?"

"I think it's normal."

Kate continued, "I have given up on that idea of a fairy tale wedding, or happily ever after. It may sound like a cliché, but I want to make the best of each day. Derek is on board with that, so all is good."

"I'm happy for you."

"Same here," Kate said.

Since they were already late, Ellie had to hold back what was on her mind. Kate was understandably still reluctant to invest more in her relationship with Derek—but Ellie was a romantic at heart. She wanted a true happy ending for everyone.

Chapter Seven

After a busy morning, Ellie didn't have time to call Derek until she was back at the department, heading for the upper floor to see what delicacies Detective Doss had brought. As she entered the room, she realized he wasn't there. She waved to Jordan who stood with Doss at the far end and quickly tried his number.

This time, she reached him and got to ask about Fiona.

"How is she?"

"Last I checked, she was pretty shocked—turns out one of the guys put something in her drink. It's now up to Narcotics, but they'll let you know if you need to ID anyone."

"Okay. Thank you."

"She's lucky you were there," he said. "She said to tell you she's grateful."

"It's no big deal."

"Oh, it is. You caught it. By the way, is Jordan anywhere near?"

"Yes. Give me a second, I'll get her."

Ellie walked across the room to join Jordan and her colleague. "Derek for you. Hi, Maria. I hope you don't mind Jordan invited me."

"No problem. Help yourself, there's plenty."

By the time Ellie got herself a coffee and a chocolate-covered donut with sprinkles, Jordan had already ended the call and handed the cell phone back to her.

"Everything okay?"

"We're not sure," Jordan said. "He seems to have trouble matching his schedule with his informant's. The guy has been fairly predictable so far...Sprinkles, huh?"

"Yes. It's been a great day so far." Concerns regarding the serial killer house notwithstanding, but they'd handle it like everything else—one day at a time.

Jordan's smile was answer enough.

"Admit it, being this close to work is really convenient—leaves you time for all the important things."

"Believe me, I see your point. Okay—now this is going to be interesting."

Both Derek and Bethany arrived at the same time. He nearly slammed the door in her face. Ellie exchanged a look with Jordan, thinking she'd give him the benefit of the doubt. Derek Henderson was a pretty even-tempered guy, though he hadn't forgotten Bethany's conduct in the Darby case. Come to think if it, none of them had.

"You're all here, good." Bethany cast a longing look at the box of donuts. "I wanted to come by in person and thank you all for your contribution. Ellie, you've helped a lot. Deane and his people are now our responsibility."

Despite enjoying the flattery, Ellie couldn't help overhearing the whispered conversation between Derek and Jordan.

"Of course they are," he muttered under his breath.

"Be nice."

Henderson shrugged and went to get a snack, exchanging a few words with Doss in the process. Ellie turned her attention back to Bethany, curious.

"Just like that? Lilah is already in?"

"We had to move up our deadline, and there was an opportunity. So again, thank you guys. We'll be in touch."

Given what she'd seen in the bar, Ellie was wondering if the Prophets would rein in their sons if they knew what they were up to outside of the compound, or if the exact same thing was going on inside. Except the women in there had nowhere to go.

Thinking of the dangers Lilah might be facing, her assignment didn't seem like something to aspire to anytime soon—even though, if successful, it could make her career.

Ellie would focus on her own path.

In the afternoon, she was back in the squad car when the alarm of a store in the city center was triggered. She answered the call and after only five blocks down the road, she arrived at the address where a woman, the owner, she assumed, stood in front of the shattered show window.

"Thank you for coming so quickly," she said. "Officer…Harding. They're gone."

"Are you sure?"

"Yes. This," she pointed at the broken window, "and the door is the only way they could come in. I swear, I'm going to kill him. No, actually, please, pretend I didn't say that. I'm going to sue his ass for every last cent though."

"You are?"

"Sherry Irwin. I own this store."

"And you have an idea who did this?"

It wasn't until now that Ellie realized exactly what store this was. The mannequins in the window wore lingerie, but sexy underwear wasn't all you could buy here.

"I know who did this," Sherry Irwin claimed as she opened the door with her key, and they stepped inside. "My ex hates it. I think he can't decide if it's because I'm successful, or because he thinks there's a special meaning in the theme, if you know what I mean. Well, both are true. He wasn't the greatest lover."

Taking a closer look, Ellie realized that the robbers had cleared out a few shelves of products. The cash register seemed untouched.

"Ed knows I take my break around this time. People either come early, or in the afternoon or evening."

"Did you hear or see anything?"

"Just the noise when they broke the glass. My apartment is upstairs. I called 911 after the alarm when off and then stayed inside for a few minutes longer."

Ellie cast a look through the window at the other side of the street. There were a few offices. Maybe someone had seen the robbers from there.

"Do you have a security camera?"

"You bet. Come upstairs with me? I'll show you a picture. I'm sure it will be him and one of his buddies in the video."

"Why steal the merchandise?"

"Honey, I appreciate you trying to keep a straight face," Irwin said dryly. "It's not for personal consumption, believe me, though maybe he should try it rather than come up with those petty schemes. They're going to try and sell it online."

"Well, we're definitely going to take a look at that. I'll get some colleagues in here so we can check for prints, and I need the security footage."

"Just a second and thank you. Everything is so much better when someone is actually doing their job. Look, Ed wants to embarrass me, knowing I now have to deal with the police and the local press maybe. Guess what—I'm not embarrassed. I improve many more lives than he does selling insurances to people who don't need them."

"Speaking of insurance..."

"Yes, I'll call mine," she said. "You're going to dust for fingerprints like on TV?"

Ed, Edward Rollins, quickly lost his salesman smile when Ellie identified herself.

"Sherry is crazy. I wouldn't want to go anywhere that 'business' of hers. I don't want my name associated with hers in any way."

"So, you didn't resent her for opening the store?"

"Your wife divorces you and opens a sex shop, what do you think people said behind my back and to my face? Of course I resent her for that, who wouldn't?"

Ellie suppressed a sigh. Eyes on the prize. Tomorrow afternoon, she and Jordan would be on their impromptu road trip.

"I don't know who broke into the store, but it wasn't me. I don't need what she's selling."

"All right. The footage from the security camera is being analyzed right now, and we found prints. I assume you have nothing to worry about."

"You assume correctly, Officer," he said.

"Thank you for your time."

"No problem." He studied her for a moment. "Listen, I know you're young, but I imagine your job can be dangerous at times."

For a brief moment, Ellie wondered whether he was going to threaten her.

"Do you have children? Have you thought about life insurance?"

"Again, thank you. I need to go."

When she was out of earshot, she couldn't help but say the words out loud.

"I can't believe this."

It would have been nice, though, if there had been nothing but an elaborate prank gone bad behind the break-in, something to be resolved quickly. Too often, reality was a lot darker.

Nevertheless, she'd have to go back and browse the sites that Sherry Irwin had given her to see if someone had put up a new batch of sex toys. If she was lucky, she could take a quick look before anyone noticed and then check with the lab if they had anything new from the security camera.

The few officers present were all going about their work when Ellie arrived. Wes Martin from her class was conducting an interview. She would seize the moment. She doubted that whoever had stolen the items from Irwin's store would put them up right away, but maybe, hopefully, they were exactly that careless. If anything, she could check out the sites and find out where new sellers would put their merchandise.

Ellie considered herself fairly open-minded, but her search made her face grow hot. *To each their own...* She sensed someone come up behind her and decided on a pre-emptive strike.

"I don't want to hear any jokes, okay? This is work."

"Don't worry, Harding, I wasn't going to suggest anything else," Sergeant Bristol said dryly.

Ellie swiveled her chair around for face her supervisor. "Sir, I'm sorry. I thought..."

"I can imagine. Any leads so far?"

"The ex-husband denies he did it. I was going to see someone in the lab about the security footage, then we'll know more."

"Good. Hm. Not every day that browsing those sites is part of the job."

"Well, I don't really do it at home... I mean...I'll go to the lab now," Ellie said quickly before the situation could become any more awkward.

The lab technician had some good and bad news for her. The camera had caught the robbers, wearing masks and gloves as they emptied whole shelves within minutes. Neither of them seemed to have the ex-husband's build or demeanor. Before leaving the store through the broken window, one of them held up a piece of cardboard, the word *Bitch* scrawled on it.

"Classy," Ellie remarked. Even though Sherry had insisted it could only be her ex, Ellie was inclined to believe him. He held a grudge, for sure, but he didn't seem so specific about it as to come up with a plan like this.

Later that day, Jordan was nowhere to be seen. Ellie decided to go home and get in some study time before making it an early night.

She wondered how Lilah was doing, cut off from the world.

The thought made her shudder. The vacation she'd had with Jordan had gone a long way towards healing for both of them, but some of the nightmares lingered, and would for a long time to come.

Before going to bed alone, she typed a text meant for Jordan, but then didn't send it.

Tomorrow was almost here. She had to be sensible. What could happen between then and now?

Between the two of them, they weren't counting favors. When Derek asked her to meet with his informant tonight, a man called Mac who had helped them break a case not long ago, Jordan couldn't say no. There were many places she'd rather be than driving out to the address he'd given her, Ellie's bedroom on top of that list. The scenario she imagined was rather innocent. She was tired, and the idea of curling up next to her after a long shower was highly appealing—maybe she could still do it after talking to Mac who claimed he had something important to say after standing Derek up a couple of times.

He knew it would be her, and he hadn't been too thrilled about it, but finally relented. What he had to say was too important. Derek hadn't specified why he couldn't go, but he didn't ask favors like this often. The area wasn't too bad, just one broken streetlight that she'd seen, the front lawns mostly well kept. At the end of the road, the houses were farther apart, but still in acceptable shape. She parked in the spot Derek had described and walked towards the front door of the one-story house. It was empty, its former owners victims of the housing bubble. No one had come back here to develop the area much, but prices were still too high for many to take on necessary renovations. She didn't think Derek would send her to a house where she'd risk breaking her neck. Jordan knocked on the door and walked inside.

"Hey, Mac. I'm here."

She sighed when silence greeted her. What was up with this guy? A look to her watch told her that it was five minutes to the time they'd agreed on. If he didn't show up, then maybe Derek would have to reconsider the merits of working with him.

A quick check of her surroundings turned up nothing particularly alarming—lots of dust and spider webs. There was a door leading out to a patio. She opened it, wincing at the sound cutting through the silence of the night.

This didn't feel right. No matter how much Derek trusted this guy, he had acted strangely these past few days, more skittish than usual. She had a random memory of negotiating with Darla who had a keen sense for danger. Whenever she suggested it was better to back away, she was usually right.

Derek hadn't even told her what was so important that this meeting absolutely had to take place—chances were, he didn't know details either.

Jordan turned to the living area again. The blow came out of nowhere, making her stumble. Fortunately enough, it caught her in the shoulder, and she got to her feet quickly enough to catch a good glimpse at her opponent. Not Mac, she assumed, before he lunged again, but this time, she was better prepared. When he was down, she had a moment to reach for the cuffs, but he kicked her hard, jumped up and ran. Seconds later, she heard the engine of a car from the back of the house and let out a curse. Somebody must have been waiting for him.

It looked like whatever important information Mac had to deliver, he'd been made first. She reached up to touch the side of her head, wincing. This was a warning more than anything else, but she could have done without it. There was nothing much she could do tonight, but she sent a text to Derek, informing him that he'd better check in with his CI, as he wasn't the one who had shown up.

Jordan drove home, for the first time annoyed with having to drive to the other side of the city. It was too late to call Ellie, wake and probably scare her, so she went straight to the bathroom, stripped, and threw the clothes in the hamper. The small cut on her temple had stopped bleeding. The bruise on her shoulder would be quite colorful, but she could cover it up and prepare Ellie gently.

After a quick shower and changing into PJs, Jordan decided she was entitled and made herself a Gin Tonic she drank on the couch. She had meant to go to bed, but at some point, she fell asleep, her dreams a weird carousel of people, familiar and unknown.

"I need you to listen to me," Kathryn said. She had a gun in her hand.

At 3:47 a.m., Jordan was jolted out of her sleep, realizing she was still on the couch, the empty glass sitting on the coffee table. She went to brush her teeth, trying to shake the vivid image of a desperate Kathryn. If she was lucky, she'd get a few more hours of quality sleep.

The images kept haunting her. Unnerved, she gave up around five, willing to start the day in the hope that the afternoon would come soon.

⌘

"I'm sorry I couldn't make it, sounds like this was a waste of—what happened to you?"

"Didn't you get my text? I told you, someone else showed up," Jordan said. "The good news is, I don't think they meant to kill me, or you, for that matter."

"You left out a few details. That bastard!" Derek who had been sitting behind his computer with a coffee, jumped to his feet.

"It might not be Mac's fault. Whatever he meant to tell you, someone didn't want him to."

"Yeah, well, that comes with the territory. I'm going to find out what's up with him. I'm really sorry."

"Don't worry. I'll be off for the weekend in a few hours, so that's my incentive."

Going about her work, Jordan had almost forgotten that she had another appointment before she could get Ellie and drive out of town.

Kathryn was already there when she made it to the bistro, seven minutes late.

"I'm sorry," she said, then almost regretted it. With Kathryn's history of showing up late—or not at all—when Jordan needed her most, there wasn't much she had to apologize for. Certainly not for seven minutes.

Jordan had been under the impression that this was what Kathryn wanted, seeing her on a more regular basis—and Jordan might have hoped that if she saw her again, her long-held anger would change to something else, less heavy to carry.

Nevertheless, their encounter started off with awkward silence.

"You got hurt," Kathryn finally said, sounding fairly concerned.

"It's nothing." Her tone was final, communicating that she didn't want to go into details, and fortunately, Kathryn took the hint. The waitress came to take their orders, giving them both another opportunity to stall. Jordan thought of when they'd last met, the intense and emotional conversation that had her call Ellie and ask her to come just so she could remind herself that her life was so much better now.

"So, how have you been?" she asked eventually.

"Okay." Kathryn shrugged. "I'm happy that you wanted to see me again."

"Shrink told me it's good for me." Jordan couldn't help it. "You got all those tests done? Got your meds?"

"Most of the time. I feel better now."

"That's good."

Back to silence.

The salad she'd ordered wasn't half bad, but Jordan's appetite was fleeing. What had she imagined? She and Kathryn had their big conversation, meant for closure and moving on—maybe there was really nothing more to say.

"Things are good for you too? With your girlfriend?"

"Yes. In fact, I'm off from work until Monday—we're going on a little trip."

"That is so nice. I'm glad you can have the life you chose. I really am."

For the longest time, Jordan had thought she was the main reason Kathryn couldn't have a life of her own choice, until she truly understood how irrational those thoughts were. Words like these brought them back easily.

"I worked hard for it," she said. It was true, but the guilt lingered. Did you still have a responsibility to take care of your parents when they had never really done you that favor in the first place? She'd had a roof over her head, and food most of the time. Unless Kathryn or Jim forgot to buy some, because they were too high, or the money had run out. Closure wasn't done easily or quickly.

"Do you need money?"

Kathryn's face fell. "What do you want me to say? That wouldn't be a good way to start over, would it?"

"No. I'm asking anyway."

"I told you, I manage most of the time."

Jordan opened her wallet and counted off six twenty-dollar bills. "There's something I need to take care of. Could you please pay for the salad? Thank you."

"Jordan, please stay. I don't want your money. All I wanted was..."

"I'm sorry. I can't do this right now."

She was handling the situation. Jordan thought ruefully it didn't mean she was handling it well. Thank God for the long weekend. She had a headache. She'd let Ellie drive.

Chapter Eight

W hen she arrived at Kate and Ellie's apartment, she found Ellie sitting at her laptop, the packed suitcase on a chair next to her.

They both did a double-take, Ellie, when she first saw Jordan, and Jordan when she caught a glimpse at the site open on the screen.

"You got special plans for the weekend?"

"No, you first," Ellie said. She got up and walked over to Jordan, lifted her fingers to gently touch her temple. "I saw you yesterday afternoon. When did that happen?"

"Just something freaky. Next time I'll think twice before I go see one of Derek's CIs."

"You did report it though."

"Derek will take care of it. I'm more curious about your internet research."

"Oh, that." With a sigh, Ellie glanced over her shoulder at the laptop. "It's about work. Someone robbed a store in town...No one was hurt, but the owner thinks they're going to sell stuff on the Internet."

"They stole a bunch of sex toys? I don't think this week can get any more bizarre."

"Tell me about it. So, you're ready? How did it go with Kathryn?"

Jordan shrugged. "Okay, I guess. I believe I've done my part."

Ellie put her hands on her arms, before she said, "You've done more than that. Let's have our little time-out. We deserve it."

All of a sudden, Jordan felt self-conscious about the way she'd ended the conversation with Kathryn. It could have been worse, right? If Ellie knew, she'd only be worried. There was no reason. This would be the last time she'd put money into the equation.

"We definitely do. Now tell me a little more about the research you did. You find anything interesting?"

She laughed at Ellie's self-conscious expression. "Don't worry. I'm kidding."

Lilly was a lost sheep desperate to be found. After less than a week, she already fit perfectly into her new community—so well that the woman sitting on a barstool, drinking her troubles away, almost didn't exist anymore.

She always was one of the first at prayer, she always did her chores with a smile on her face, and she had accepted the clothing and hairstyle. Not that it changed much, in his opinion. He could easily see past the infantile dress and hairdo that all women were supposed to wear so they wouldn't tempt the men or distract them from more important subjects.

Lilly, he thought, couldn't help herself. She was flaunting her perfect body and her easygoing personality, and no matter how hard she tried, she would always struggle to stay pure. Some women were like that, and they needed a strong hand to keep them on their path.

There would come a time when she would have to make a decision. Sadly, he wasn't the one who could choose her. It made him angry. So much anger he always had to suppress, because it wasn't his turn, because one of the brothers came before him.

He would end up with someone lesser, more flawed. If Lilly was that person, he wouldn't mind, but for now, he kept watching her.

She was friendly, but he saw through her spiel.

Jennifer had been friendly too.

The weekend was flying by much too fast. Since there was no saying when they could plan their next vacation together, they had decided to splurge on the hotel room by the lake, spa included. Jordan didn't mind Ellie tending to her in various ways either—and she didn't even have to play up the bruises to make it happen. Jordan liked the quiet of the woods around them—it reminded her of her home. No matter what sacrifices she made in terms of commute, they were worth it. They were sitting out on the deck with a cocktail, and even now Ellie was reading through some papers in a folder.

"Are you sure you will remember those?" Jordan asked skeptically. She vaguely remembered freaking out over test preparation.

"I know I will. I'll do it more intensely once I get closer, but for now, I just want to imagine those scenarios in my mind." She frowned. "Actually, most of those, I don't want to imagine, but you know what I mean."

"Yeah." Jordan leaned back in her chair, happy to let go of all catastrophic scenarios, real and imagined.

The peaceful moment lasted about ten minutes, then her cell phone rang. Ellie looked up from her folder. "Don't tell me you were going to bring it in the hot tub."

"I kinda hoped if I brought it, it wouldn't ring."

Jordan picked up the phone and answered.

"Hey, what's up? You have two minutes."

"That's enough," Derek said on the other end of the line. "I talked to a few people, and I've arranged something with Mac for Monday afternoon. I thought you might want to know."

"Sure, thanks. Did he have an explanation for bailing on me?"

"Not really, but he says he has something big. You know the kind of people he got us before. I'm thinking it might be related to Dr. Roberts' case."

"Why do you say that?" Jordan sat up straighter in her chair.

"Someone in the area is stockpiling weapons, as it seems. I'm not sure if he has anything more, or if it's related at all, but it would be a big coincidence. They're not sure what is coming, but they want to make sure they're prepared."

"That's a really optimistic outlook. Sure, yes, I do have some questions for him. This is where you're going to say I shouldn't tell Bethany?"

He made a dismissive sound. "That's up to you, but if this leads to something, and you want it on your résumé rather than hers, you should consider not telling her yet."

"All right. I'll think about it. Your two minutes are up."

"How's the air up there?"

Jordan looked over at Ellie who was immersed in her study material once more.

"Perfect," she said. "Come on," she added after ending the call. "The hot tub is waiting."

Ellie didn't hesitate.

❧

By Monday afternoon, Ellie was successful in her quest for the stolen sex toys. She found every item Sherry Irwin had reported to her on one particular site, all on sale from the same vendor.

A couple of calls with customer service and then, a manager, confirmed that they would need a warrant to release the details of HotStud69's account.

She looked around, wondering if she could convince anyone else to knock on A.D.A Esposito's door, then decided to be brave.

Esposito called her in right away.

"Officer Harding, hi. How can I help you?"

Ellie had a moment of irrational sentiments before she cleared her throat and laid out the situation to the A.D.A. who, much to her credit, listened to her all the way.

"There's nothing on the security footage to tie the ex-husband to the robbery, and the prints weren't his, so this would really help."

"Sure, I can see where you're going with this. Let me make a call, and I'll let you know when it's all ready."

"Thank you."

Was it her imagination, or was the woman's gaze lingering a bit too long?

"You're welcome. Is there anything else?"

"Um...no. Thanks."

Ellie left the office, willing herself to forget about Jordan's past sins.

Even Bethany had admitted it—she had won.

By the time the warrant came through, Ellie couldn't reach anyone at the Secret Pleasures site—she still considered the day to be a successful one. First thing in the morning, she'd get the vendor's name. She was looking forward to sharing her progress with Jordan, preferably over a beer at the *D&T*. However, her call went to voicemail, and when she ended it, another one came in.

At first, she didn't recognize the voice and wondered if the caller was mistaken.

"Ellie, it's Darla. Do you have any idea where Jordan is? I really need to reach her."

"I don't know, I was trying to reach her myself. Can I help you with anything?"

Darla hesitated.

"Please, tell me. I'm off from work now."

"I really hate to ask, but I have a job interview this evening. They made time for me out of the regular office hours, but now my babysitter came down with something—I didn't know who else to call."

"Why don't you come to my apartment? I'll meet you there."

"Really? I don't want you to think I'm not handling this. I am. This is an exception."

"No problem," Ellie assured her. "I can take care of him for a couple of hours."

"That's amazing, thank you so much."

"I'll hang up now, but I'll be there in ten minutes. See you then."

She arrived only a few minutes before Darla pulled up in front of her apartment building and headed downstairs quickly to help her with the bag she brought while Darla carried the baby, a boy named Jordan Avery.

"Let's call him Avery around here," Darla suggested, "to avoid any confusion." They both laughed. "Seriously, that means a lot to me. If I can get this job, I'll earn more, and it gives me so many other options. You're the best." She hugged Ellie quickly.

"I told you, it's no problem. Good luck and go get them!"

Then Darla was gone, and Ellie realized with a feeling between amazement and panic that she was alone with a baby. An hour, two max. They'd be fine, right? Avery was on the verge of falling asleep, yawning adorably.

"You are too cute," Ellie told him. "I think I could get used to this."

Jordan had a hard time understanding what the trouble had been, as Mac met them in the park in plain daylight.

"Sorry that didn't go so well," he said with a quick look to her, prompting Derek who had been silent and brooding during the drive, to react.

"You son of a b—"

"Derek. Henderson, come on, stop it."

"I swear, it's not my fault," Mac insisted. "I was going to call, tell you it was too dangerous."

"You were being followed?" Derek asked, still not in a forgiving mood.

"I didn't think I was, but man, this is all bad news on top of bad news. There's been a lot of money exchanging hands lately for guns, from people who don't want their names to pop up in a background check."

"Is that so? What kind of people?"

Mac shrugged.

"Come on."

"I can't say it's related to those nutcases that keep their girls on a short leash, but I've heard the name Beaumont dropped."

"Anything to suggest that it might not be Raphael Deane who killed her? Or about a book?"

He shook his head. "I don't know anything about a book, but one of the guys had a leather bag—I think they make them there."

That, and jewelry boxes. "Thanks, Mac," Jordan said. "That's very helpful."

Derek shot her an incredulous look.

"Now I'd like to hear a bit more about those gun sales. Did anyone approach you personally in the past few days? Did they know you were going to meet me instead of Derek?"

"Hell, I said I don't know!"

"So you really have nothing," Derek observed. "It might be time we go separate ways then."

"Hey, I helped you with that crazy kid who blew up the bar, right?"

"You're not helping right now."

"Okay. There's this bar. I hear they sometimes let them out on the weekend or something. They're not supposed to drink, I think, but no one says anything if the men do it. They hook up with the working girls as well, and it's a place where people offer the merchandise."

"Oh crap. I know the place. Mac, there's someone I'd like you to meet."

"No way," Derek said. "If there's any whisper he's been talking to the Feds, he's dead."

"He's talking to us now, isn't he? I can set up something low-key with Bethany."

"I don't like it."

Mac's expression said clearly that he didn't like it either.

"Wait here," Jordan told him. "Derek? This is important," she said after they'd walked a few steps, keeping Mac in sight. "They have a company that's dealing in leather ware. The sooner we can prove what their real intentions are, the sooner they can get their agent out."

"Her well-being is Bethany's responsibility, not yours."

"Oh, for Christ's sake, she made a mistake and nearly got me killed, I get it. I was there, remember? I'm not sure what's up with you but stop it. I'm going to call her tonight."

"I can't guarantee that he'll show up."

"Yeah, we've been there." She held up a hand when Derek was about to protest. "We're good. Hey, Mac. Don't leave town."

Jordan wasn't sure what Derek's plans for the evening were, or if she even wanted to deal with his cranky mood any longer. They both drove to the station to finish up on their respective workdays, and she didn't see him again until she pulled out of the parking lot and noticed his car behind hers. Oh well. She'd make that call to Bethany quickly.

She was first to arrive at Ellie and Kate's apartment—apparently Derek had taken another turn or had stopped at a grocery store.

When she heard the sounds, she momentarily thought she was in front of the wrong apartment—but it was definitely Ellie's voice.

Ellie, as she noticed walking inside, talking to a baby.

"This was definitely a success," she said. "Not the fun part, but a success."

"Did I miss anything?" Jordan asked, amused. "When did this happen?"

"Well, it was time for changing, and I thought to myself how hard can it be?" Ellie chuckled. "That's not what you're asking. Hi."

"Hi."

They shared a quick kiss before Ellie laid the baby down into his carrier.

"You were busy, so Darla called me instead. She had a job interview but couldn't find anyone to take care of him."

"Thank you for this. Derek and I finally met his elusive informant."

"You did? Did he have anything good for you?"

"Promising," Jordan said, remembering she still had to make that call. "Excuse me for a second?" Or maybe she didn't want to discuss details with Ellie at this moment, which would disrupt the unexpected, cozy scene.

Bethany picked up right away. Jordan could hear a female voice in the background, asking, "Who is it?"

"Work," Bethany said. "It won't be long. Right?"

"I don't think so. Can you come in tomorrow? There's someone I want to introduce to you. He had some news about the Prophets of Better Days case. Not all good, but it might be helpful for Strickland. Apparently, they are stockpiling weapons from the black market, and the name Beaumont was mentioned, not in connection with Raphael."

"And that person is trustworthy?" Bethany asked doubtfully. "You don't think Raphael killed her?"

"Oh, I know he did, that case is solid. But we might get closer to proving that the family put him up to it."

"I'll be there. Thank you. See you tomorrow."

When Jordan returned to the living room, Ellie was sitting on the couch with Darla's son in her arms.

"You want to hold him?" she asked.

After a moment of hesitation, Jordan nodded. She laughed self-consciously. "I'm not sure how this will go. The last time I held a baby, they threw up on me."

"Relax. I don't think that's going to happen every time."

They heard the key in the lock, and a moment later, Kate and Derek walked in.

"Okay...This is new," she remarked. "Something you didn't tell us?"

"It was news to me," Jordan said. "He's Darla's. She'll be picking him up in a bit. You guys brought beer?"

"You called Dr. Roberts?" Derek asked, obviously in a better mood now.

"I'm going to see her tomorrow. I promise, we'll do this the right way."

"Tomorrow's going to be a big day," Ellie remarked. "We'll finally find out who stole the sex toys." Even though her tone was serious, everyone burst out laughing, in the process waking Jordan Avery who made small happy baby noises.

Jordan was both intrigued and spooked.

This was not the time.

❦

To her surprise, Bethany caught up with her early in the morning, intent on joining her for roll call.

"I want you guys to focus on the gun sales," she told Jordan on the way. "No word on Lilah."

"Is she doing okay in there?" Jordan didn't have any update on the woman Ellie had rescued, but it seemed like the brothers and their sons weren't strong on impulse control. If they started assaulting and harassing women when on the outside for five minutes, she hated to think about what was happening on the inside.

"So far, so good," Bethany said. "I'd like to pull her out rather sooner than later, so if you can get Henderson's informant to meet..."

"He's reluctant, but I think he'll do it."

"Make sure he does. I don't want to take any chances."

Derek would be pleased to hear that. Hopefully, he could convince Mac too.

The address Ellie and Casey Lyons pulled up to was an old warehouse that had been converted for office space. As they entered the building, they noticed that most of the offices were empty. There was a private investigator on the first floor, and a computer repair service on the second. The repair service was closed. The PI opened the door to them.

"Officers, how can I help you?"

"We have a warrant for Jack Smith under this address."

He frowned. "Well, it's not me. I've been in this building since they first started renting out, and I don't think I ever met a Jack Smith in here. There's a computer firm upstairs, and an insurance broker just moved in. Real estate company coming next month. Maybe it's one of the employees?"

"We'll check that, thank you," Ellie said, turning to Casey. "Insurance...Irwin's ex owns an insurance company. I wonder if the two are connected."

"Let's find out."

They only found the secretary who confirmed that there was no Jack Smith working for the company. She didn't know Irwin's ex-husband either, but she could give them the name of the landlord, a company named Modern Local Development. A quick check revealed that this company also owned the building where Irwin had his insurance business.

Too much of a coincidence?

They had barely fastened their seatbelts when dispatch alerted them to shots fired only a few blocks away from their location, two people injured, the shooter fleeing from the scene.

Ellie wondered if Jordan, who had been mostly silent when she'd come to roll call with Bethany, was having a better day. She could only hope. They arrived shortly after the ambulances, sirens competing. Libby, who was already on the scene, told them what she knew.

"Male, white, late twenties, pulled a gun on a woman. When someone tried to help her, he shot him too and ran. Male victim's got a flesh wound, but he could describe the shooter."

"What about the woman?"

Libby looked somber. "Doesn't look good. We should make the call."

Ellie cast a look at the woman on the stretcher, to the blood staining the concrete, and back. "Damn." She would have liked to use a stronger word, but the realization came like a gut punch—she knew the woman.

"Fiona Grayson. The man, was he with her?"

"No, he was just a bystander," Libby said. "More backup is on the way. Let's send a detective to the hospital too."

With all necessary measures taken, Ellie and Casey joined the search, and at the same time, warned residents to stay inside. While it looked like the shooter had targeted Grayson specifically, he had already injured another person and likely wouldn't hesitate to do it again.

They were combing the neighborhood, house by house while the description was going out to all officers on patrol.

Ellie had a hard time forgetting the image of Fiona on that stretcher, wrestling with questions she had no way of answering at the moment. Had she been targeted for talking to the police about the incident at the bar, or did she know more about the Prophets? Were the gun sales Derek's informant had talked about, related—had she known about the book?

"Pay attention," Casey snapped at her.

"Sorry," Ellie mumbled, knowing that Casey's criticism was perfectly justified at this moment.

"What's going on?" a woman called from a first-floor balcony.

"Ma'am, please, please go inside. We're looking for a man who ran from a crime scene. He might have a gun."

"Well, good luck finding him. That sounds like most of my neighbors. Forget I said anything, most of them are just paranoid, or so I thought, but now that you're looking for..."

"Ma'am. Please," Casey stressed.

"All right, all right."

Fortunately, the woman stepped back into her apartment and closed the curtains. They had almost made it to the end of the street. Behind, there were woods and fields, another team on the lookout.

The last house had a wooden gate leading to a backyard. It looked like no one was home. There was no car in the front. The mailbox was nearly flowing over.

Ellie wanted to curse again, but this time, she had no words. The gate stood wide open. Chances were the owners hadn't left it that way.

"He might be long gone," Casey said quietly.

Or he had noticed that the way the teams had been set up, they were closing in on him, Ellie thought.

In the backyard, a swing and outdoor furniture were protected by plastic covers, one more hint that the owners had likely prepared for their absence.

One of the chairs was turned over. There was a small shed nestled against the fence around the property. They carefully edged closer to the shed, noticing that the lock and its windows were intact.

Both of them rapidly ducked for cover behind the small building when a shot rang out.

It was coming from inside the house. Casey called for backup while Ellie tried to get a glimpse of what was going on inside. The sun was almost blinding, but she could see a shadow moving inside, a man pacing. Would he come outside, try to shoot his way to freedom, or move the other way? He had to know that the house would be surrounded within minutes.

What kind of weapon was he carrying?

Seconds later, Ellie had her answer, and it was the worst possible. He came out shooting, advancing on them with every step. Both she and Casey had their guns drawn.

"Police! Put your gun down!" Casey yelled, then ducked when her words were returned with more gunfire. As he was coming closer, they had no chance but to return shots.

One of his bullets hit the shed's wall, bits of brick flying around. Ellie could hear Casey curse. She raised her weapon again, and then the shooter jerked, dropping to the ground.

He didn't move.

"Ellie. Ellie, are you okay?"

"I suppose," she said, feeling sick as she turned to Casey, startled at the smear of blood on her face.

"It's the damn brick," Casey said. "I'm okay, it's nothing. Cavalry is here too." Several officers had come from inside the house, one of them taking the rifle out of the shooter's reach, another kneeling down to reach for the man's pulse, shaking his head.

Ellie took a deep breath, feeling light-headed and a tad confused. Had she killed him? It was entirely possible. She had fired her gun at the same time as at least one of their colleagues who had backed them up from the inside. One of those bullets had found its mark. She was relieved that none of them were hurt, save a few scratches from flying brick...she thought she might be sick.

"Breathe," Casey advised as they walked over to their colleagues. "It will be okay. You had no choice."

Ellie knew this for certain, but that didn't mean she had accepted the fact yet. At her first look at the man, she involuntarily took a step backwards.

"She's a beautiful girl, don't you think? Why does she have to draw attention to herself, being dressed like that?"

"His name is Seth," she said. "I don't have a last name, but I'm sure he's with the Prophets of Better Days. I talked to him at the bar...he said he was married." Something inside their sect was unraveling, and fast. The man who had slipped something into Fiona's drink, hadn't come after her, but one of his fellow cult members had. Ellie felt her throat go tight. She had no reason to feel sorry for Seth who had obviously attempted to kill Fiona and injured another person—but she imagined the wife he left behind, probably young, mother to a few children.

"Ellie! Thank God you're okay."

Jordan's embrace was brief, but it was enough to do away with some of the confusion. This wasn't about her and her feelings.

"Hey," she said, wondering why Jordan was here, but grateful for it. "You might want to get Bethany in on this. He was the guy at the bar who talked to me and gave me his opinion about Lilah's clothes. Unless he lied to me, he had a family." Ellie shook her head. "One he didn't seem to care about much if he put the brothers' secrets above them. What a shame. I mean...I would have preferred if I didn't have to shoot him," she added quickly. "I had to. He kept coming at us."

"We'll figure it out. No one's going to blame you for that. He was coming at you, it's a clean shot." Jordan's expression, however, showed concern.

She stood a little straighter, as if pushing against a weight on her shoulders.

"Did you go to the hospital?"

"Doss went," Jordan said. "Fiona Grayson is still in critical condition. The witness is doing okay."

That was a bit of a relief. There was still hope for this day—and Fiona.

"Okay. How do you think they will react? I don't assume they will easily accept that this was his fault to begin with?"

"Probably not. Do you want me to drive you?"

Ellie shook herself. "No, I don't think so. I'll go with Casey. I'll see you later, and...thanks for coming."

Jordan's smile was slightly pained. "I had to," she said.

Being in the same room with Derek and Bethany was uncomfortable and awkward. At the moment, Jordan couldn't care less.

"Mac mentioned guns on the street, and a group that's probably with the brothers looking for large quantities that don't show up on background checks. One of those guns might have ended up in the hands of a guy who decided to shoot two people earlier. The serial number was scratched off," she explained to Bethany.

"I want Mac in here. Arrest him for loitering, anything that makes him look innocent and harmless and not like a snitch." That part was meant for Derek rather than Bethany. Jordan turned back to her. "Meanwhile, we have to go see Daniel Deane again."

Seth, as it turned out, was Raphael's half-brother, from Daniel Deane's third marriage. Of course, wives number one and two still lived on the compound with their children and grandchildren. Whatever the women's opinion was on how the brothers ran the family and the business, they would not welcome the police.

They had to be careful not to alert them and jeopardize the operation in progress. The reason why they could identify him so quickly, was partly due to their earlier surveillance.

"It's not going to be easy," Derek warned. "After this incident, Mac will want to lay low."

"Don't we all," Bethany said sarcastically. "The thing is, we don't have that luxury. Strickland's life is on the line."

"I'm aware. Regardless, I can't promise anything."

"Just try," Jordan said. "We're on the same side here, remember? We don't want to tip them off, but we need to move fast before more people get hurt. Derek, you call me the moment you get a hold on Mac. Meanwhile, we have to deliver the bad news."

At least, no one protested. Jordan was comforted to know Ellie was safe somewhere in the building and probably would be for the rest of the workday...On a day like this, Jordan had even less patience than usual for Bethany and Derek's mutual resentment.

Chapter Nine

H e couldn't help being excited, even though he knew it was very, very bad. Both Nathan and Seth had been courting Lilly, regardless of the fact that Seth's wife was five months pregnant with their fifth child.

He had watched the cops come to their house, again, and the Prophet answering them with his grief and fury...

He wasn't grieving though, not that much anyway, and if it was wrong, he couldn't help it. What had happened, would put him higher in the hierarchy, and closer to Lilly. He'd be smarter than Seth, too, who had volunteered to clean up the mess Nathan had made with the whore at the bar.

Eventually, the Prophets would understand that he was worthy, unlike the men who snuck out to drink and hook up like college girls, or Seth who'd been falling over his feet to be helpful and screwed it all up.

Or Raphael, who was behind bars and would likely spend the rest of his life there.

He would do better because he was more deserving than the rest of them.

His reward was right in front of his eyes, every day.

There was no more doubt that Lilly would want to stay. He'd be able to start his legacy with a wife and children of his own—and the biggest lever in the game, Jennifer Beaumont's elusive work. That could go either way, give it to the brothers, or the police...He'd bide his time, listen, and find out who wanted it more, and what they could give him for it.

It was in an uneasy mood that Jordan and Bethany returned from the compound. They'd been met with the usual suspicious looks, men having their—legally bought—guns on display. It was unnerving to think that they were trying to get their hands on many more, in sales that they thought couldn't be traced.

Daniel Deane had been rather calm and stoic when they told him the news. They didn't get to see Seth's widow as women and children once again remained hidden from sight.

Thinking of them made Jordan feel sick, too many unwanted reminders that came with that. Of Ellie's abduction, of Darby's basement. Those women might not be in immediate mortal danger, most of them, anyway, but they were trapped nonetheless, no way out. The children grew up with a harsh distinction when it came to the rights and tasks of boys and girls. They wouldn't know anything else...unless the authorities managed to do more than stop a few of the brothers' sons. If they could stop them all.

She could understand why Bethany took the risks she did. Darby was serving a lifelong prison sentence. They could bring down the brothers as well and send a message to every group that might want to start something similar.

"He's going to sue, isn't he?" she said out loud.

"I'm sure," Bethany said grimly. "The department, the FBI—I'm sure his lawyers are coordinating strategy right now, but they won't get far. He was shooting at cops, refusing to drop his weapon. There is no way this could have gone any differently.

I hear Harding kept her cool under fire. I can kind of understand why you like her."

Jordan shook her head. "Not the moment."

At a red light, Bethany laid a hand on her arm. "It will be okay. There's nothing she needs to worry about."

"Except one thing."

Bethany didn't argue. Jordan was lucky she'd never had to shoot to kill, but she'd come close, and she'd known colleagues who had to cross that line.

No matter how justified her actions were, this would be hard on Ellie.

Ellie had a conversation with Sergeant Bristol which assured her even more that she'd done the necessary, if not easy thing. It seemed trivial in comparison, and so she had almost forgotten about Jack Smith and his connection to Sheila Irwin's ex-husband. However, the robbery had presented a substantial threat to her person and business. Ellie didn't want to fail her even on a day like this, so she went to see Esposito once more.

"Those are interesting findings," the A.D.A. said, "but certainly not enough to arrest him. Why don't you have a detective look into that, dig some more into his company? I think you should have done that a while ago, no offense."

"None taken. You're right. Thanks."

On her way out, she ran into Kate for the first time that day after the shooting. Her friend enveloped her into a spontaneous hug. Ellie could guess what was going through Kate's mind right now.

"I'm okay," she said. "He didn't get that close."

Kate stepped back, looking self-conscious. "That's what I heard. Wow, I'm sorry. I just..."

"I know. It's okay," Ellie assured her. "I think Jordan will be here a little while longer, but I could really use a drink. What about you? Is the *D&T* okay?"

It seemed like the *D&T* would be their replacement hangout for now. Owned by a gay couple, it had a somewhat mixed audience on any given night.

"Sure," Kate said without hesitation. "They have the best happy hour in town."

Having opened only a few months ago, they already had an excellent reputation.

"Okay, that's settled then."

Ellie sent Jordan a text to let her know where to find them in case she wanted to join them later. Half an hour afterwards, she and Kate sat at the bar, both with tall glasses decorated with umbrellas in front of them.

"That was really cute," Kate said, referring to Darla's baby. "It's cool that she named him after Jordan."

"Yeah. But you only came in after I changed the diaper."

"Obviously you were successful." Kate laughed. "So, have you and Jordan talked about—"

"Come on!"

"I mean the housing situation."

Ellie shook her head. "Come to think of it, we did talk about children. It's an option, but this year, we have so many other things on our plate. I don't want to take the exam just to see if I can do it—I want a few more years on the job before we go there."

"Sounds like you've given it some thought." Kate sounded wistful.

"What about you?" Ellie asked.

"Absolutely no. For me, that falls into the same category, marriage, kids, making plans that never come true. I enjoy life the way it is, more than ever before. If you stop investing so much, it takes a weight off."

Like the last time they'd had this conversation, Ellie disagreed, but she figured neither of them really knew better. She just knew what felt right.

"Derek feels the same about it?"

"He's not trying to persuade me, and I appreciate that. Oh look," Kate said as she turned to the entrance. "Now that's interesting."

Ellie followed her gaze and quickly picked up her glass, taking a sip.

"None of my business—or yours." She couldn't help but cast another glance at Bethany Roberts who had come in with another woman. Ellie suppressed a sigh. Bethany did have a type, not that she could blame her.

Come to think of it, those were rather trivial musings given the situation she'd found herself in earlier today. Ellie didn't want to think about it. Tomorrow, they'd have the ballistics report, and she was certain it would confirm the bullet had come from her gun. She'd have to go through the motions, but she had little doubt she'd be cleared—why didn't she feel more relieved?

"I'll have another one," she said, lifting her glass. "You?"

"Sure."

Ellie was halfway through her second when Jordan entered the bar. She stopped briefly by Bethany's table, and they exchanged a few words, before Jordan joined them at the bar.

"Hey, I see you already got started. Would you like to share an appetizer? I don't know that those peanuts are going to carry me through to tomorrow morning."

"I'm so glad you're here. I love you," Ellie said. *Oops*. All she'd meant to say was, *hi*, and *of course I'll share something with you*.

Come to think of it, she and Kate had started on an empty stomach. But there was always a reason, wasn't there?

They decided on a plate of nachos, a portion for two that was more than big enough for three.

"How are you doing?" Jordan asked.

Ellie shrugged. "Right now? Pretty good. I don't know about tomorrow, but I figure it will be okay."

"Bethany and I had a chat with Derek's CI earlier. That gun Seth Deane used was unregistered, probably one of the sales he was talking about."

Ellie frowned. "That doesn't make sense. They are so secretive, according to the FBI, and now they keep screwing up. He comes after her in broad daylight, with a gun from a shady sale they are trying to hide?"

Jordan shrugged. "Daddy Deane is not happy. I got the impression that had less to do with one of his sons being dead, and more with the fact that he made them look bad—well, worse than the usual."

"So, we're no closer to finding whether or not they told Raphael to kill Jennifer, or if it was his own plan all along. Frankly, I'd prefer to know he's locked away forever, and that's it. Girls, would you mind if we quit the shop talk for a little while?"

"No objection from me," Jordan said with a questioning look to Ellie. She picked up Ellie's glass, took a sip and told the bartender, "I'll have what she's having."

For some reason, that made her crack up and come dangerously close to crying...but everything would be okay. It had to be.

Lilly had tried for most of the day to comfort a grief-stricken Mary Ellen, with little success. She had even skipped some of her chores for that. Mary Ellen, in a desperate situation with no income, four children and a fifth on the way, was relieved from hers for the day.

He'd been watching them, once again thinking how stupid they were, Seth, Nathan, Raphael, getting imprisoned, killed, or dancing on the edge of either one.

He knew what he had to do, and that he had to be patient to get it. They were laughing at him because he never wanted to come with them to the bar, meet random women. He knew they were making fun of him behind his back, wondering out loud if he might still be a virgin.

Sometime soon, he would earn the brothers' trust, and show everyone that he was a true soldier who could carry on the way of the Prophets.

Jordan wasn't surprised to find Ellie crying when she returned from the bathroom at Kate and Ellie's apartment, ready to turn in for the night. She curled up beside her, holding her tight, aware that there weren't any words that would make Ellie's worries vanish into thin air. They had to wait it out, adjust to the new situation. It was a good thing they had both become pretty good at that.

Ellie's reaction wasn't just because of highly unlikely consequences. Today could have turned out to become so much worse.

Maybe, she pondered when Ellie had long fallen asleep beside her, she had been wrong to brush off Kathryn as she had. The Kathryn of the present anyway, maybe she did deserve more of Jordan's consideration, and words. She might see her again,

113

if only to find out if she'd used the money for medication, or something else. She wanted to be sure before she invested too much in that relationship—it hadn't turned out so well for her the first time.

She shifted her thoughts back to the job. Fortunately, they had managed to bring in Mac and let him go without fanfare, and they were a little closer to tying the Prophets to the gun purchases.

Now, Lilah Strickland had to make contact. If that worked out, they might even find the elusive book.

The next morning brought a roller coaster of emotions for Ellie. As it turned out, the bullet that killed Seth Deane didn't come from her gun, but that of a member from another unit backing them up that day. After trying to come to terms with the possibility, this news threw her off for reasons she couldn't explain to herself.

"Be glad," Casey advised. She was still sporting a Band-Aid on her temple from the pieces of brick that had hit her face. "It's a lot less paperwork for you that way."

"Do you think I did everything right?" Ellie asked, feeling self-conscious and at the same time, strangely detached. "You still got hurt."

"Come on, don't go there. It's a scratch. It's a lot less than it would have been if he'd gotten to us. We, you were lucky that the guys moved in at the same time—otherwise it would be you with all that paperwork."

"What if I couldn't do it? What if I had choked?"

"You didn't. You made the right call. Come on, Ellie, you're a good cop. If you don't believe me, ask Jordan—or the woman you rescued from her neighbor's basement. Should I go on?"

"Please, don't. I get it. It's just...odd. I was almost getting used to the idea, and I'm not sure what that makes me."

"Someone who wants to stay alive. Someone who wants their partner to stay alive. That's a good person in my book." Casey was well aware of Ellie's emotional state, because she added, "If you're looking for something to make you feel better, stop at the new coffee shop on Third Avenue. If you'd like to make *me* feel better, you can pay."

Unwittingly, Ellie had to laugh. "That's easy."

"Told you." More serious, Casey added, "You did everything right. If I remember correctly, Bristol told you too. I'm grateful we're not in that kind of situation every day, but you did good yesterday. Let it go."

"I'm trying." Ellie guessed that for today, it was the best she could do.

Jordan didn't know what had possessed her to drive by the trailer park that evening after a largely uneventful day—something everyone was grateful for after the shootout with Seth Deane. Everyone went about their job, and there was no news from the family or Bethany.

She was asking for trouble.

When she walked up to Jim and Kathryn's trailer, she was struck by the changes since she'd last been here. A fresh coat of paint. A small table with two chairs that looked like they, too, had been painted. A freaking flower box.

Had she been too harsh and quick in her judgment? If that was the case, who could blame her? Expecting the worst had usually served her well.

"Hey. Jordan. It's good to see you here. I made coffee. You want some?"

"No thanks, I won't stay long."

Jim Larson's face fell a bit, but he caught himself quickly.

"Is Kathryn here?" She couldn't let herself be lured into this polite, friendly exchange, the pretense that nothing bad ever happened. Still, Jordan had to wonder whether she would have been better off thinking that Jim was her father rather than the career criminal TJ Pratt.

"No, she went out to see a friend. Would you like to wait?" he asked even though she'd expressed her visit would be a short one.

"I don't have that much time. If you could tell her I stopped by...?"

"Sure."

"Would you mind if I used the bathroom?"

"No, of course not. Come on in."

Stepping inside, Jordan was immediately hit with the feel of claustrophobia. The smell of air freshener couldn't offset the memories. The last time she'd been in here, there had been no time for that kind of sentimentality, as TJ had been holding Kathryn hostage. Now, she was spooked, by Kathryn and Jim's attempts to turn this place into an actual home decades too late, by what lingered under the surface.

She locked herself in the bathroom and opened the medicine cabinet, looking through the different bottles of medication. Something to counter high blood pressure, pain meds, and surprisingly, anti-depression. Some that she didn't recognize.

All together, they would cost quite a bit—so Kathryn had told the truth. Maybe that was what she had needed, to test her, to find out if the tiniest bit of trust wasn't misplaced as it had been most of the time. Jordan leaned back against the door, taking in the clean room, again, the smell of air freshener, and a scented candle. She didn't know what to make of it, or how to feel about it.

When she stepped outside, Jim stood at the small kitchen counter, filling his coffee cup.

"Are you sure you don't want one?"

"Absolutely." She was about to leave, then turned around, opened her wallet and took out a fifty. "Could you give this to Kathryn? Thank you."

She didn't stop to explain to a stunned Jim Larson, already feeling caught in a trap she had built for herself.

Adding to that, there was a sense of guilt creeping in, for potentially betraying Jack and Pauline who had given her a family when her own parents were incapable of taking care of her. Irrational, maybe, but she couldn't help it. When it came to holding on for all the wrong reasons, she had some dubious skills...but everything was changing. Ellie in her life was changing everything.

Chapter Ten

E llie spent most of her afternoon dealing with a car accident—a hit and run, in which fortunately no one got injured—and a small fire that was set by a drunk neighbor who confessed on scene. The last call came from a woman whose boyfriend had pulled a knife on her out of the blue. Like the amateur arsonist, he was drunk but showing a lot less remorse. She had to jump aside, or he would have spat on her.

"Precious," Casey said as they put the cuffs on him. "Makes me want to go back to the coffee shop."

"I can't. I have plans." Ellie didn't want to go into details as they were still on the job, but she was looking forward to dinner with Jordan and the couple she considered her real parents, the ones who had shown up for her.

Jack and Pauline were kind and easygoing people, and Ellie felt comfortable with them. They were also fairly interested in grandchildren. Who knew? She and Jordan might make that decision.

Casey had brought their charge to the car, while Ellie assured herself that the woman, a college student named Beth Jeffries, was all right.

"He didn't hurt me, thank God," she said, shuddering. "You arrived at the right time. I hope he's not going to get out so soon."

"Did he do anything like that before?"

Beth shrugged. "He gets a little intense when he drinks—but he never freaked out like that before. Something he saw on the news, I think. This is it. I'm going to change the locks on him."

Ellie didn't blame her, though she hoped this was really the last time either of them had to deal with him—given the circumstances, he might be out not long from now if no malicious intent could be proven. She wondered about Lilah Strickland, risking everything to prove that the Prophets weren't all that holy, but dangerous criminals and abusers instead.

"Is there someone you could call to come over, or stay with tonight?"

"Yes...I think I'm going to call my friend. He's really staying in jail overnight?"

"Yes, you don't have to worry about that. You can call that friend now? I can wait."

That earned her a small smile. "Thank you. I didn't know you guys did all that."

Ellie didn't tell her that she'd feel bad going back to her own, almost perfect life without making sure Beth was taken care of. She wanted the day to end on a good note.

When she made it to Jack and Pauline's house, Jordan was already there, the family having a cocktail outside on the deck. Pauline got up to get her a glass, and Ellie followed her.

"Thanks so much for having me tonight. I have to ask though, is there any special occasion?"

They'd had dinners with Jack and Pauline before, usually on a weekend. It hadn't occurred to Ellie until now that this exception might mean it was an anniversary or someone's birthday.

Pauline gave her a surprised smile. "I was going to ask the same question—not that I mind. I figured you both had a long day and were not in the mood for cooking."

"More like a couple of such days. We're really grateful," Ellie said, wondering if there was something Jordan had yet to tell her.

"It's no problem." Pauline opened the fridge and took out a bottle of rosé wine, then she poured a glass for Ellie. "In fact, we love having you here. I know you're both busy, but we've seen more of Jordan since she's with you. It's been good for her...and there are a lot of questions I want to ask, but I swear, I'm not going to."

"We haven't made any plans regarding kids yet—but we babysat for a friend once."

Pauline laughed. "I'm sorry I'm this predictable. We're just really happy for Jordan—for you both."

Ellie thought that a little over twenty-four hours ago, she and Casey had been seeking cover behind that shed. Jordan's idea had been the perfect one.

"I am very lucky," she said before she picked up her glass, and they went back to join Jordan and Jack.

During dinner, everyone did their part to keep the conversation light, and later that night, Jordan joined her once more at the apartment. Maybe it was because of Ellie's little meltdown the night before, or this was a sign of bigger changes to come. Either way, Ellie was glad for the time they had together after yet another turbulent few days. Kate wasn't home. If she was honest, tonight, Ellie was grateful.

"I really enjoyed tonight," she said.

Jordan sat on the couch, legs pulled up under her. "Me too." She didn't offer any further explanation.

"I had a nice conversation with Pauline in the kitchen. She was thinking we might have some announcement to make."

"Hm."

"I do feel kind of silly though, for losing it last night. I mean...It wasn't even my gun."

"It was still dangerous, and you held it together when you needed to. That's all that counts."

Jordan sat up straight, putting her feet on the floor. Ellie curled up beside her, lying back in Jordan's lap.

"I'm glad you think so. I don't even know why...There's been a lot going on."

"No kidding."

Jordan's hand gently brushing over her hair was almost hypnotic. If she closed her eyes, she might fall asleep—but that wasn't Ellie's intention. "I have the feeling that's not all though...?"

Jordan was silent for a long moment, then she sighed. Another pause, before she said, "It's about Kathryn."

Of course it was. Ellie hated to be suspicious of people she didn't know. She had enough information about Jordan's birthmother to be cautious at best.

"What did she do?"

"Actually, it's not something she did. I gave her money. Twice," Jordan said with a tone so resigned Ellie sat back up.

"She asked you for money? When?"

"She didn't ask for it, but when we met, she mentioned that she had trouble paying for her meds. It's true, she takes a lot of them...I know because I went to look through her medicine cabinet today."

"What?"

Jordan laughed wryly. "It's not as bad as it sounds. I didn't break in. She wasn't home, but Jim was. I asked to use the bathroom."

"Okay," Ellie said, beginning to understand.

"Now I'm not sure if I've been stupid and fell for their scheme, or if thinking that would make me a horrible person...but it's not even that important. I'm glad you're okay.

I'm glad the bullet didn't come from your gun, because that's something you grapple with, even when you have no choice."

It might still happen, Ellie thought. Of course, Jordan knew it too.

"Did you ever...?"

"No. But I came close, too."

There wasn't much time to consider the implications, the ringing of a cell phone jolting her out of her thoughts. It was Jordan's.

"I'm sorry. I think I have to take that."

"It's okay." Ellie didn't assume that Bethany would call at this time of day if it wasn't work-related. At least that's what she hoped.

Jordan listened for a moment, before she said, "We'll be there."

"We as in you and me?" Ellie asked, perplexed, when she had ended the call. "Where?"

"The place where she's going to meet Agent Strickland."

Ellie didn't need any more time than the two seconds it took to grab her keys. "Let's go."

Jordan was surprised to learn that Strickland had made it off the compound, and she assumed the young agent had enough information for the case—most likely, multiple cases—to go forward. Going back in would be too dangerous, especially under the circumstances. What she saw at the address Bethany had given her worried Jordan. It looked like a family home from the outside, a two-car garage, a wrap-around porch with a swing in the front.

Russo was with them. He let Jordan and Ellie in, and they followed him upstairs to a spacious office space. At the table,

Bethany sat with Agent Strickland. They were talking in hushed tones.

Jordan was struck by the young agent's transformation. She looked tired, older, an impression only enhanced by the shapeless, greyish clothing mandatory for women living with the Prophets of Better Days.

"Agent Strickland has done amazing work," Bethany said, nearly glowing with excitement. "We have plans of the building. Now it's only a matter of time."

"It's as terrible as anyone can imagine." Lilah Strickland shuddered as she addressed Jordan and Ellie. "Actually, it's so much worse than I imagined. You wouldn't believe this is going on right under our noses. They teach the kids the absolute minimum to pass tests, but frankly, I'd be surprised if all of those kids were registered at all. They start working on the farm at a young age, and they tell the boys that they can rise in the hierarchy if they marry early, even become one of the Prophets one day...they consider girls to be of age at fourteen. I have spoken to a number of engaged, or already pregnant teenagers, and the older women..." She shook her head. "You can imagine."

Jordan could, after seeing what only two weeks in that place had done to Lilah. She could tell from Ellie's troubled gaze that she was having similar thoughts.

"You have documentation?" she asked softly.

"Most of it," Lilah said. "It's pretty damning on its own, but there are several things happening right now. They are wrapping up another big gun purchase. Everyone is already tense, because of what happened with Raphael and Seth. Both of them wanted back in the brothers' good graces, but they achieved the opposite with drawing attention to the family. In any case, they'll move all the children into the school area on that day, so they'll be safe. On that day, you'll get all those assholes and the gun sellers too."

"Sounds like a win-win," Bethany said. "They won't see us coming."

"Yeah," Strickland agreed tiredly. "I'll have to go soon. I befriended a woman who helped me—she thinks I'm just going out to have a drink and a cigarette," she said, laughing wryly. "This place is insane. I look forward to putting most of them in prison for a long time. The women—they'll be free for the first time in their lives, but sadly, not even all of them will see it that way, that's how conditioned they are from a young age."

"Wait, you're not going back in?"

"I don't have a choice. If I disappear now, they know something's up."

Jordan looked to Bethany in disbelief, but she didn't get any help from her.

"The woman you were talking about, how do you know you can trust her? If she's as conditioned as the others, this might be a trap."

"I think I can trust my judgment, Detective. It's not without risk, but I know that if I can hold out for a few more days, I can give you a lot more. Meanwhile, your idea paid off. Here's some additional reading material."

She put a USB key on the table.

"Jennifer Beaumont's book. Happy reading."

When confronted with expectant looks, Lilah Strickland said, "Once I knew where to look, it wasn't all that hard. Remember, Jennifer used a box from that store to send the bracelet to her mother. Nathan Deane owns the company, but it's his wife, daughter and other girls on the compound who produce most of the merchandise they sell on the Internet. My friend knew where she hid it. She's been living in fear ever since. If we do this right, so many women and children will have a future."

"And what if they're on to you?"

She caught Ellie's thoughtful look. For sure, she wasn't making this decision, but Jordan had a bad feeling about it.

"I am doing my job," Strickland said briskly. "I understand it's a matter of interdepartmental courtesy that you and Officer Harding are here, just so you have a heads-up for what's to come. I strongly suggest that you leave the rest to me and my supervisors."

Much to her credit, Bethany didn't gloat.

"I agree. We have a lot of work to do now, go through the material Lilah gave us," she said. "Then there's the book. We'll prepare a joined operation over the next few days, so when she gives us the go ahead, we can go in and catch those bastards in the act. Their lawyers will twist and deny the facts best they can, so the illegal gun sales are a bonus for us. People are a bit more sensitive these days."

"The sale will happen on Monday, no later than seven PM."

"How are you going to contact us?" Ellie asked. "I assume they monitor your communication."

"I'll send you Deborah," Lilah said. "I want her and the kids out first."

"We'll make it happen," Bethany assured her. "We'll make it all happen."

Chapter Eleven

B ack at home, Ellie brewed a pot of tea, and they sat at the
kitchen table, both of them still absorbing what they'd
heard and seen. Jordan felt apprehensive at the thought of div-
ing even deeper into the world of the Prophets of Better Days,
from the view of the women trapped on the inside. Ellie looked
pensive.

"I hope Lilah makes it out safely. That's a lot of responsibility,
sending her back in there."

"Strickland's cover is still intact. She knows what she's doing,
and Bethany does too."

"I imagine she thought the same thing when she was exchanging messages with a serial killer, offering up her girlfriend
as bait!"

Derek overheard the last part of Ellie and Jordan's conversation when he and Kate returned to the apartment. Even if he
hadn't, Jennifer Beaumont's book was open on Ellie's tablet:
Imprisoned. Given the task at hand, Jordan had no desire to
discuss Bethany's competence with Derek.

"Jesus, not this again. And keep it down. People are asleep in
this building," she said, not bothering to hide her exasperation.

"You have to go to her supervisor over this. Someday soon,
she's going to get someone killed, and it might be Agent Strickland."

"Come on, don't be melodramatic." Jordan tried, but she couldn't help the feeling that Derek had a point. He didn't like Bethany, but even taking that fact out of the equation, she knew there was a high risk.

"I can't interfere with any of this now. It's not just Bethany—Russo and Strickland agreed as well. They have some material, but catching the good brothers trying to amass enough guns for the zombie apocalypse will shut them down for good. There are rumors Jeremiah and John might be present. This is going to be big."

He shook his head, exasperated. "Wow. I can't believe the things you're ready to excuse with this woman."

"Hold on a second." Ellie who stood leaning against the counter, had followed the conversation silently until now. "I was there. It's true what Jordan says."

"Yes, you were there, and I wonder about that too. What kind of game is she playing?"

"There's no game," Jordan said. "They're all doing their job. Would I prefer Strickland had wrapped this up before she left? Sure. But it's not my call, and it's not yours."

"You feel good about this?" Unfortunately, he knew her well enough.

"No. There's nothing we can do about it now. They're going to set something up—we'll see if they need us or not."

He scoffed. "What do you think?"

"I think I'm tired, and I don't want to discuss this with you any longer. I have a book to read too."

"That's unbelievable," he said, turning on his heel the moment Kate returned from the shower. "I'll see you tomorrow," Derek told her. "Bye."

"I guess that means no staying over," she said with a sigh. "All right, what is this about? I heard you arguing from the shower."

Jordan glanced at Ellie, imploring her silently not to tell the truth—not yet, in any case. Kate would be interested in the book—she had been the first officer to talk to Jennifer Beaumont's mother about her missing daughter.

"Just work," Ellie said.

Kate looked doubtful. "Are you okay? I want to be sure I'm not walking into something tomorrow..."

"It will be fine." Jordan got up and snatched Ellie's tablet from the table.

"Didn't I hear something about Agent Strickland?"

"We talked about her earlier, wondered how she might be doing."

"Okay then." Kate yawned. "I'm going to bed."

"Yeah, that's a good idea," Jordan said quickly. Ellie nodded. They were both curious and apprehensive about what Jennifer Beaumont had planned to reveal in her tell-all. It had to be something so dangerous to the Prophets of Better Days cult that one of them gave the order to murder her. If they were lucky, she had named names too.

Beaumont's writing was clear and concise, engaging even though she dealt with disturbing numbers and facts. It was even more chilling to know she would not live to see the men committing these crimes arrested.

Jordan noticed that Ellie had stopped reading. She didn't blame her. It was the stuff of nightmares, and God knew they both had enough of those already. She couldn't help sparing a thought on Darby who claimed he'd been teaching morals to the women he'd murdered. Or Josh Ward, who had teamed up with Ellie's kidnapper, hoping to exploit the situation. Misogynists. Killers. It turned out the Prophets had men like that in their midst, unrepentant abusers who thought they had the right.

"That's really bad," Ellie said somberly, leaning back against the headboard. "You were worried about Lilah earlier."

"It's a high when you're getting this close. I hope she won't be careless."

"I didn't think she was. Like you said, all we can do now is wait."

"Yeah. That's what I don't like."

Ellie put the tablet aside, turned off the light and wrapped her arms around Jordan.

"It will be okay, all of it. I promise."

How could she argue with that?

❦

The feeling of foreboding didn't go away, and Derek's sullen mood didn't help. Lilah's information, as well as Beaumont's writings did help to piece together the motive for Seth Deane's shooting spree. Apparently, a group of men left the compound on a regular basis. The fact that they asserted complete ownership of their wives and children didn't seem to count. They wanted more, drunken binges, sex with random strangers.

This was a part the brothers didn't approve of, and married Seth had known it. By attacking Fiona Grayson, he had wanted to prove himself as a soldier of their group, but all he'd achieved was to draw more attention to the cult.

Jordan had to admit Lilah Strickland was right in one thing—it was unbelievable that the brothers had managed to stay under the radar for so long, under the guise of a religious community, a handful of entitled-feeling men creating a dystopian world just barely out of the city. In fact, it took years of planning, purchasing real estate, upholding a tight hierarchy through intimidation.

"I'm sorry. I didn't mean to call your judgment into question." It had taken him nearly the whole day, but Derek had finally come to that conclusion.

"That's okay."

"This case is messed up, and a lot of people already got hurt. I will admit I have a hard time trusting her."

"Bethany isn't the only one who signed off on this, and Strickland knows what she's in for. She wanted the weapons deal to go down, and the children out of the way. As much as I didn't like her going back, that was something we could all agree on."

"I guess. You're coming over tonight?" he asked. "*Night Shift* or *D&T*?"

After last night's meeting and reading time, the mere mention nearly made her yawn.

"None of the above. I haven't been to my house in three days or so. I need to make sure no one stole the bills from my mailbox."

He chuckled. "I think you'll be safe. Have a good night."

One of them had surely overreacted, Jordan thought as she drove through the city, eventually taking the exit that would take her to her neighborhood. In her case, it might be that she'd never forgiven herself for not catching on with Darby's intentions right away...but her instincts had been right on the money, warning her that there was something strange about the always present son of an ex-cop, or the rich and entitled children of a murdered businessman. She wasn't exaggerating. While she had to let Bethany and the other agents do their jobs, it didn't mean that she had to like it.

As she got closer to her destination, the traffic flow continued to improve, and the quiet drive made her once more aware of the unresolved situation. She wasn't yet ready to give up this space. There was no denying though that she spent the better part of the week at Ellie's, had taken up a corner of her closet, and enjoyed the shorter commute to work. Shortly after the Darby case, everything had felt too close, too personal, too claustrophobic.

Now, she was motivated to do her job, but the separation was clearer, easier. This wasn't her story. She wasn't trapped any longer, the realization starting to sink in. Maybe that would help her make a more permanent decision, though she had no idea what plans Kate and Derek might have for their future.

Jordan parked the car in her usual spot. She was about to get out when something made her stop in her tracks. When she eventually got out, she cautiously looked around, but everything was quiet. Upon closer examination, doors and windows were intact, no locks broken. Taking in her front door, she made no effort to keep in the expletive. She turned around to see if the neighbor's car was in their driveway. It wasn't. The couple might still be at work, though Jordan didn't know what their jobs were. One of the reasons she liked it here was that there wasn't any forced socializing.

It was highly unlikely that she could even find the person in question, but she'd file a report anyway. Jordan took a picture with her cell phone and unlocked the door carefully. No footprints or tire tracks anywhere near. Said person had walked up to the door, did what they wanted to do and quietly driven away. It was minor in the grand scheme of things, and Jordan had seen some pretty scary things in that grand scheme.

Still, it was annoying and a bit unsettling, the graffiti scrawling over the door in giant letters: BITCH.

"Do you see why we should be living together?" Jordan gave her a tired smile, and Ellie filed it away as a success. She wasn't going to press the issue right now, but it was hard to deny, a change of plans good and bad always led to a lot of extra driving. Like now. Jordan had assured her that she didn't need to come.

Ellie had multiple reasons to be here, one of them being the strange coincidence of some people scrawling gendered slurs on available surfaces. Was this connected to the break-in at Sherry Irwin's store, or did misogynist minds think alike?

"Yeah. If we did, maybe I could make you paint the door."

"A.D.A. Esposito told me I should let a detective handle this, and she was right. So I did, but I have no idea what happened."

"It's worth checking," Jordan agreed, not commenting on the fact that Ellie had been talking to Esposito. She was still critically taking in the front of the house. "Come to think of it, it could use a fresh coat of paint all around. The deck, too."

"Whoa, one thing at a time. First, we want to find the 'artist,' right?"

Jordan shrugged. "I will file a report, for all the good that will do. I've been called worse."

Ellie studied her for a moment. "You know, just because other things might have priority now, it doesn't mean this doesn't matter. You're still worried about Lilah?"

"A lot depends on her—and Bethany making the right decisions."

"Yeah...Look, why don't you get your mail and some fresh clothes, and I'll drive you to the station. Then we go home, make it an early night? I don't want you to be all alone in the haunted house."

A split second later, she wished she could have taken back those words, but Jordan didn't seem much fazed by them.

"Sure," she said. "I might have to use your washer too."

"No problem," Ellie said quickly, relieved she hadn't crossed a line. Baby steps. For now, they had other mysteries to figure out.

❦

The connection between the robbers and the person vandalizing her front door still remained unclear after Ellie had talked to the detective on the case.

At least, the case against the Prophets, from the department's side, was coming together. Fiona Grayson expressed that she was willing to testify when Jordan saw her in the hospital. She did so when Ellie was on her lunch break, so they could compare notes afterwards. Jordan thought that it probably did Ellie some good to see Fiona was doing better...and it might distract her from other things. The term "haunted house" hadn't gone unnoticed. Jordan didn't want to get into that conversation until she knew exactly the right words to say.

There was no "if" anymore when it came to Ellie in her life. The "how" was still something they had to figure out, and with Ellie studying for the upcoming detective's exam, it might not be a good time to tackle those questions.

"There have been a lot of stories about that bar, and members of a group who call themselves the Prophets of Better Days. The man who shot you was one of the sons."

"Yes, the married one." She shook her head, winced. "Well, I guess most of them are. They come to that place because the audience is discreet. Not any longer, as it seems, so some of them got cold feet. For sure, I'm never going back. First, they slip something in my drink, then they try to kill me. How much stupid bad luck can one person have?"

Jordan caught Ellie's thoughtful gaze. There wasn't really a limit, but that wouldn't be of any help to the woman.

INITIATIONS

"Oh, and I hear you saved me twice, Officer. Thank you."
"You're welcome."
"Are you at least going to arrest some of them?"
Hopefully soon. Hopefully all of them.
"It's an ongoing investigation," Jordan told her. "Be assured, your statement helps us a lot."
"Well, I have to do something right at some point in my life, don't I?"
She wasn't going to argue with that. If only the "haunted house" problem was solved this easily. Then again, maybe she was overthinking this.
"Thank you, Ms. Grayson. If you need anything else, or remember something, please let the officer in front of your room know. You can always call me, too." She left a card on the woman's table.
Grayson made a tired salute.
Jordan and Ellie went on their way, stopping at a diner for a quick bite.
"Did you hear from Bethany?" Ellie asked when they sat in a booth.
"No. I assume it would be any day if they need department resources."
"Okay. I guess they told Raphael that we found the book. It's so strange and scary to think that Rhonda was dating him. They are beyond the pale...hating the women who follow their rules so much that they cheat on them and hating the women on the outside for not following their stupid rules."
"Real class acts," Jordan agreed. "The good news is that there'll be many arrests coming soon. Between Strickland, Raphael's case, and Seth Deane shooting at police officers, their cult will get a good shake-up. If we're all lucky, they won't recover from that."

135

"Are they aware of that, or are they just this ignorant not to notice? It scares me to think that they might have some apocalyptic plan B."

"I've been thinking about that too." There was no reason to deny Ellie's worries, when they were this obviously justified. "Bethany and her people know what they are getting themselves into. The weapons sales are disconcerting—it's a question of how paranoid they truly are."

"They don't have to be this paranoid—the existence of their cult is threatened for real."

"Yeah." Jordan sighed. "I don't mean to distract with something utterly profane, but there isn't much we can do as long as the FBI is taking the lead on all counts. And I really need to buy some paint. Might as well do a big job with the front."

"You really want to invest a lot of money in that house?" Ellie was trying to sound neutral, or so Jordan assumed, but a hint of disappointment came through.

"It is fine for me now, but I'll have to spend some money if I want to get a good price for it someday. What? I never said I wanted to grow old there. I know you're not particularly attached, and I..." That was the harder part. "I just bought it," she finished, aware that she wasn't explaining anything. "It's not haunted, just like the *Code 7* wasn't. We'd go if it still existed."

"That's kind of the point, isn't it? It doesn't. It's okay. I'm fine where I am now, and as long as you are...I'll be waiting."

"Sometimes, I think you are so much better than I deserve," Jordan said ruefully, meaning every word of it. It wasn't like the past few months had been easy for Ellie, yet she was still here, patient.

"No." Ellie smiled. "I am exactly what you deserve. I'm afraid I have to get back to work now, but if you want, we can go to the hardware store after your shift. I'll help you paint the whole house if that means you're going to sell it some day."

That was more than a baby step, Ellie thought, absent-mindedly filling out reports. Jordan was so cautious to the point it could be irritating, or at least it had felt that way at one point or another. After everything they'd been through, individually, together, Ellie understood their respective approach. She understood Jordan had her reasons to be cautious. Even if she refused to vilify Bethany, Ellie knew Jordan's ex had played a part in this, and so had Kathryn, her birthmother who was trying to make amends extremely late.

So, selling the house eventually was an option. Ellie had promised Kate that she wouldn't move in with her only to leave again after a few weeks—that wasn't likely to happen. There were new possibilities though.

Thank God. She could be patient, give Jordan the space she needed, but she would be happy when they could lay that particular subject to rest. For sure, Ellie had her own unresolved issues, even though she did a fairly good job distracting herself from them. She wanted to be a good partner. She knew Jordan's history with Kathryn was still a touchy subject, probably always would be.

Ellie realized she hadn't gone to her parents' graves since before being attacked one night on her way home from the *Code 7*.

"Harding, do you have a moment?"

Detective Doss's voice jolted her out of her disconcerting thoughts.

"Sure. What is it?"

"Irwin's ex finally caved and told us about the guys he paid to vandalize the store. He confessed to paying your HotStud69 to arrange the robbery with a couple of his buddies. He wanted to embarrass his wife, didn't plan on them selling the merchandise on the Internet. They're here now."

"Oh, good news, thank you."

"You want to watch?"

"That sounds dirty," Detective Waters, Doss's partner, remarked as he walked by. Doss rolled her eyes. "Harding?"

"Yes, thank you. Any familiar names, or any reason why one of them would go to Jordan's house?"

Doss shrugged.

"Nothing came up in the cross check yet, but I'll ask them. I'd be surprised though if the two are related. There are too many jerks with big mouths and a too small vocabulary."

"Yeah." Ellie wondered if Doss included her partner in that category. Now that the exam was looming closer, she had to pay more attention to the dynamics between her future colleagues—at least she still hoped she could go straight into that unit.

The three men Doss and Waters had arrested earlier didn't hold back much—Sherry Irwin's ex-husband was the instigator. Each of them had been paid $2,000 upfront in return for doing some damage to the store, to get back at the "bitch" for leaving him. As she listened, Ellie couldn't help rolling her eyes too. Big mouth, small vocabulary.

"The bitch sign was a creative detail you added, or did he tell you to do that too?"

"Hey, she deserved it," Randy Wheeler, who had listed the articles under the name of Jack Smith, said. "Ripped him off in the divorce."

"Well, I'd say he ripped *you* off, because those 2K are not going to cover your legal costs, and the damage to the store. Tell me about the sign. Is that some sort of signature thing?"

"I don't know what you're talking about," he said, sounding irritated.

"I'll help you with your memory then. The graffiti on a cop's front door."

He regarded the photograph she handed to him and started laughing. "What? Just because it's the same word, you want to pin that on me, too? News flash, lady, we can't do all the work. You can ask the boys, but I don't think they go all over the city with a can of spray paint."

"I will ask them, don't worry."

Outside in the observation area, Ellie frowned. She wasn't sure if that was good news after all. If these clowns had nothing to do with the slur on Jordan's front door, who had? Her first thoughts were always going in the same direction, and she was sure Jordan had thought about it for a moment, too. The truth was, there were people who resented them for doing their job, then again, it could be completely random, some juvenile prank.

She waited until Maria Doss had finished the interview and joined her outside the interrogation room.

"I'm sorry I couldn't help you guys more. Like Jordan said, we'll probably never know unless someone catches the kid with paint on their fingers. We'll see if there are more cases of vandalism in the area, but I doubt we'll find a connection. Jordan didn't even work on this case."

"That's true. Okay. Thanks." Ellie returned to her desk with an uneasy feeling. She couldn't always expect the worst, could she? They were in a good place. She needed to trust that it could last.

Minutes later, Sergeant Bristol left his office, and to her surprise, he walked right towards her.

"Harding, I need you to come with me."

So much for trusting in the good times...

"Was there a problem with ballistics? Seth Deane?" she asked anxiously.

"No, you're fine. There have been some new developments with the overall case, though. The agents are in the house. They have requested additional personnel."

"Is anything going to happen tonight?"

He shook his head. "This is just for briefing. There is enough to go forward now."

Ellie followed him along the hallway and into the elevator where they joined A.D.A. Esposito who greeted them with a cordial smile.

The conference room was already filled, Bethany and her colleagues, detectives from the precinct, officers who would assist in the search. She saw Jordan standing in a corner talking to Agent Russo and thought that it was unlikely they'd make it to the hardware store tonight.

"Ladies and Gentlemen, may I ask for your attention." Bethany looked triumphant. "Thanks to Agent Strickland, not only do we have a complete firsthand account of the crimes committed by the Deane family, every bit to back up Beaumont's book, but we also have plans of the compound and detailed information on their weapons arsenal. We will deliver the warrant in twenty-four hours when they'll be expecting their dealers, which will mean more than two birds with one stone. With the high-profile members securing the deal, and the children in another part of the compound, we have the best chances to surprise them and nail them all for everything that's going on, from the illegal gun purchases to the domestic abuse and child abuse. They won't see it coming, but we need all of you on high alert. We're dealing with extremely narcissistic individuals who consider this a righteous lifestyle, and they are willing to defend it."

"Are they willing to die for it?" Detective Waters asked, and for the second time today, Ellie resented him—this time, he had a point, though.

"The fact that they are amassing weapons is disconcerting," Bethany admitted. "We have no reason to believe that they are preparing for the apocalypse now, but we want to shut them down before they have a chance to do so. We believe that the measures they are taking now are mostly related to the shake-up due to Beaumont and the recent incidents. Some might think they're entitled to women and booze anytime, but the patriarch doesn't think so. Of course, in his mind, he owns everything and everyone under his roof."

Daniel Deane and his brothers wouldn't be the first to believe in this idea...not everyone started their own cult, but some became domestic abusers, Ellie reflected. Some became...worse. She shuddered. This situation was bad enough. It was about time they faced consequences.

"One more thing about the children. Agent Strickland's information is as accurate as she could possibly make it, but we have to be careful."

"They might use them as shields?" This time it was Jordan who asked the question.

"They have indoctrinated them against outsiders," Bethany said.

"Make sure the little ones are safe, and that none of them gets their hands on a loaded weapon. We have talked to Child Protective Services. They are ready to assist you later with anything you need."

This case had become so much bigger than one murder that turned out to be not so cut and dried after all. Ellie felt no sympathy for Raphael Deane who had killed to cover up the crimes of his family, maybe get back into their good graces—but she could understand the dynamics that had led him there. Growing up to believe that the brothers were always right, that women were inferior and needed to be guided. The thought of the many boys and girls living with them, conditioned with the same lies, was chilling. Not that society at large did such a great job teaching children about equality.

All of a sudden, the idea of parenthood became extremely daunting—they could try their hardest, but they were up against so many obstacles. And maybe Kathryn Larson had tried her hardest too.

After the briefing, she found Jordan, and they made it to the hardware store after all. Jordan, not so much in the mood for a big renovation any longer, bought a pint of paint to cover the slur, and they headed home.

For once, the haunted house was closer to where they needed to be the next morning.

Chapter Twelve

A few young men had been assigned to secure the compound, giving up surprisingly easily when they realized they were outnumbered. Perhaps Seth's demise was part of the reason. One of them tried to run, another reached for his weapon.

Thanks to the plans Lilah had provided, Jordan, Bethany and several others made their way upstairs quickly. They came to a sort of conference room where they caught brothers John and Daniel red-handed, exchanging money with the gun sellers. There was some yelling and threatening, but they had the element of surprise on their side.

For once, Jordan was glad that the Prophets favored such a strong separation from the women and children on the compound. Within the first minutes of the operation, two founding brothers, several of their sons, and a couple of business partners were arrested. They found them in the exact same place Lilah had directed them too.

Officers were going from door to door, serving arrest and search warrants.

"You're going to regret this," Daniel Deane said to her with a small, condescending smile. "You're overestimating yourself, Detective. What do you think you're going to find? The women and children chose the quiet life here, safe from the loud and ugly outside world. They don't want to be rescued. In fact, maybe it's you who still needs a rescue after all."

"That's all interesting, but I'm afraid I don't have time to chat. We have so much more on you than you think."

Deane made her skin crawl, reminding her too much of the men like him she had encountered in her day job, men who believed themselves to be above any law. Like the serial killer who had taken an interest in her. Like her biological father.

"You mean the book that Jennifer wrote?" He laughed.

"Who told you about a book?"

"I can't seem to remember. Maybe Nathan mentioned it. It's a shame Raphael panicked and now wants to blame the family. She could have published it for all I care. We already know it's all lies, and our lawyers would have destroyed her."

"One of your sons is in prison for murder. Another was killed because he went on a shooting rampage. That doesn't bother you?"

"Oh, it bothers me all right, but that's not why you're here, is it? People like you are all about tolerance, but you can't accept a lifestyle that doesn't fit your ideas."

"Most people would have a problem with a lifestyle that includes domestic abuse and child abuse masquerading as marriage."

She went on to another room, not waiting for his answer, feeling anxious for reasons she couldn't grasp. This was going well—too well. Jennifer Beaumont's book might or might not be admissible, but there was Lilah Strickland's extensive work, the woman she had befriended, and hopefully other women who would speak out...

From the window, she could for the first time see women and children living on the compound. They would have access to Child Protective Services and therapists. Jordan assumed that even so, it would take them a long time to trust. With the numerous accusations made, some of the parents were likely to lose custody, depending on whether they were involved in "marrying" young teenagers to older men including the Deane brothers, and in other criminal activities.

Seeing the panicked look on some of the younger children's faces made her stomach churn. They were attached to even those parents who gave the term a bad name. The devil you know.

"Hey. Are you doing all right? This must bring back...stuff."

Leave it to Bethany to raise the subject right here.

"My parents weren't in a cult," Jordan said curtly.

"They were unfit, and people who cared came to take you away. That's pretty much what's happening right now."

"What's happening right now is a lot more complex, and you know it. Don't worry. I've been seeing Dr. Burns. One shrink is enough. Where's Strickland?"

"I haven't talked to her yet, but she managed to call Russo earlier. She's laying low with the other women right now. When we've cleared the place, we can take her in as an alleged witness as well."

"What about the friend, Deborah?"

"Dr. Roberts!"

They both spun around as Russo came running into the room, a couple of other agents on his heels.

"We found Deborah Deane."

No. In an instant, Jordan knew why she'd felt this was going much too well.

"What about her?" Bethany asked impatiently. "You were supposed to get her and her daughter out first!"

"The daughter is with the other children. She's safe. Deborah was shot."

"What? When?"

"She didn't make it," he said, leaving no hope. "Was already dead when the paramedics got to her. It must have happened around the same time we arrested the gun dealers."

"Damn it. She was supposed to be among the first. She took a high risk, and everyone knew it. Who do I fire before I get fired?"

He shrugged. "It was nobody's fault. The daughter was there. She said her mother had sent her while the arrests were going down on the other side of the compound, that it would be less suspicious if only one of them went to see the cops."

They headed along the corridor, down the stairs and across the yard that led to the women's day quarters.

Jordan knew from the plans they'd seen the day before that these building also housed school rooms. In one of them, Deborah Deane's body lay sprawled in front of the black board, shot in the chest. Was Daniel Deane really that bold? No, the real question was who would take the fall for this latest murder. Deborah was going to talk, and so was her daughter. All of a sudden, they had lost an important piece of the puzzle. Someone had silenced Deborah, and thirteen-year-old Ariel might be too intimidated to speak out now. The book...that stood on shaky ground, but they still had Strickland to back it up.

"Does Agent Strickland know?" she asked.

Russo looked confused.

"I thought she was with you. That's what she said in her text."

"Jordan, could you please go join the officers who are with the women and children, and find an excuse to get Lilah in here? Break it to her gently on the way but break it to her. And be careful. I have to wait here. Russo, the next time you tell me first! I want every civilian out of here now. Let's find that shooter!"

Jordan was already on her way. She knew that Ellie was among the officers on that side of the operation and wondered if she had a chance to talk to Lilah.

She found Ellie trying to assist a woman with three children under the age of five, all crying at the commotion.

"Hey. Did you or anyone here see Lilah?" She kept her voice down. The woman here had only met the agent as Lilly, a lost soul hoping to find home with the Prophets of Better Days.

Ellie shook her head. "I thought she was with you? We have pretty much everyone accounted for. She wasn't with the women."

"Just what I didn't want to hear. Someone killed Deborah Deane. We have to get everyone out of here. I can help, but I have to check with Bethany first."

Ellie looked worried, but she nodded. "Ms., I'm sorry, but we need to go. I'll make sure you and your children are somewhere safe to sort this all out. Please, come with me."

Jordan remembered her first impression of when she'd seen Strickland after weeks inside of the cult, how she'd looked tired and aged. This woman had probably spent most of her life on the inside. They were truly lost souls.

"Please, go with the officer now," she said. The woman finally relented, walking as if she was in a trance.

Jordan called Bethany to inform her that she'd assist the evacuation on this end, and that no one had heard from Lilah. This day was going downhill fast.

❦

"They're not supposed to eat this." It was the first sentence the woman had uttered since they'd left the compound for the station. Ellie suppressed a sigh. She had determined that her charge had an older daughter who was "married" to Daniel Deane, now eighteen, but obviously younger at the time of what they called the "ritual of joining spirits."

The chocolate bars Ellie had gotten from the vending machine temporarily dried the children's tears, but apparently Terah Deane considered refined sugar worse for her children's health than her daughter being with a man old enough to be her grandfather.

Knowing that Terah had grown up in similar circumstances did little to hide Ellie's irritation with her when seeing those small children, girls who would have most likely faced a similar threat if it wasn't for today's operation.

"It's been a difficult day. Could we make an exception?"

Terah shrugged. "When can we go home? This is terrible. We haven't done anything wrong. You had no right to come to our homes and tear our families apart."

"You know that is not true. I'm really sorry, but some members of your family are accused of serious crimes."

"Daniel said that would happen. It's all lies. It's because of the way we live. You don't understand."

"I'm afraid it's not a matter of understanding. These are the laws."

"I am not giving up my children. They are being raised well."

Ellie suppressed the impulse to shake her. It wouldn't do any good for either of them, realistically, but maybe it would make her feel better for a moment. Being raised well, keeping them in line with threats and abuse, while deals were made with internationally wanted criminals?

"There's someone from Child Protective Services here. They'd like to speak to you, about the general climate on the compound. It would be helpful if you talked to them."

"What are you saying? Those people have no right to—"

"Please. You can make a difference for them. We can protect you."

"He knew you would say that. If we can go home after that..."

Ellie wasn't ready to make promises.

When she went back, Jordan exited another room.

"Can you come with me for a moment?" she asked softly. "Deborah Deane's daughter is here."

"Does she know?"

Jordan nodded. "A doctor has seen her. CPS will take her later, since the father is not likely to go home tonight. Ariel still wants to work with us—that's the good news. On the other hand, no one has heard from or seen Lilah Strickland. She seems to have fallen off the face of the earth."

"How is that possible?" Ellie asked, alarmed. All of them had been busy since this morning, and she hadn't had a chance to talk to Jordan since she'd seen her at the compound. "You don't think…"

"We don't know. But so far, Ariel seems to be the only one who is willing to talk. They're looking for Strickland now," Jordan added.

Ellie didn't like her tone, the hint of defeat. They had many witnesses, but most of them would do anything to protect the family. She was scared for the young agent who had risked everything to get them the information they had. The Deanes would still be charged with illegal gun purchase, but Bethany's big dream they had shared over the past few weeks, dismantling the cult completely, was getting further away.

She followed Jordan into the room where Ariel was sitting. As she looked up, Ellie could see that her face was tear streaked. This day was too much for all of them, but especially this young girl on whom so much depended. She needed time to grieve her loss, but they couldn't give her that time.

Ellie wasn't quite sure why Jordan had asked her to sit in, but if she could help at all, she'd gladly do so.

"Hey, Ariel. I'm Ellie. Detective Carpenter says you are ready to talk to us about your family."

"They killed my mom," she said, her eyes welling up again. "Please, promise me they'll all go to prison."

"We will do what we can to make that happen, I promise. What about your dad?"

Ariel studied the tabletop as Ellie sat across from her. Jordan remained standing.

"I hardly ever see him," Ariel continued. "It's the same for all of us, and when he bothers to show up, we need to show him respect. I don't respect him. I know he hit her, and I'm sure he doesn't care that she's gone."

"I agree that doesn't sound like someone who deserves respect. Who do you think hurt your mom?"

"You can say it out loud. It's murder. She wanted to get us away from that place, and they found out. The men always say outside is a place for whores. They don't want to let us go because they're afraid we'd betray them."

"Can you tell us more about your life there, and the other families?" Ellie ventured. "It really helps us to know more. Everyone who has done something wrong will be punished."

Ariel looked doubtful. "I don't know how you are going to do that. No one ever tried. The Prophets know about everything, and everything belongs to them. At least that's what they say."

"He is married to more than one woman?"

Ariel nodded.

"Did you ever attend one of those weddings? You know that according to the law, he could only marry one person, right?"

She caught Jordan's thoughtful look, wondering if she had crossed a line.

Jordan left her place at the wall to sit with them.

"I know this is horrible. If I was you, I wouldn't want to be here. I would want to be left alone and not talk to anyone, but you're doing great. Take your time."

"I know about laws." Ariel's tone was defiant. "The Prophets say some of them are unjust and deny their greatness. I heard Brother Jeremiah has thirteen wives, and I don't know how many children. He was always in a competition with Brother Daniel. Daniel..." She swallowed hard. "He married one of my friends last summer. I was there. We all have to be there."

"How old was your friend at the time?" Ellie asked, struggling to keep her voice level.

"Fifteen," Ariel answered matter-of-factly. "We are allowed to get married at fourteen, but most of us hope it doesn't happen. Hannah has a baby now, and that's really tough. Before, it was just our chores, and we could spend time together, but now that's all she does."

"Do you know any more girls who got married recently?"

"A few. Some we take in from the outside because they were doing really badly..." She shrugged. "At least they get food and shelter here, so I guess it could be worse."

In the resulting silence, her stomach growled, prompting Jordan to get to her feet.

"Thank you so much, Ariel. I'm afraid we'll be here for a while, so why don't I get us something to eat?"

She could have pulled rank on this one, but Ellie figured Jordan was probably more than ready to leave the room for a few minutes.

"I'm not hungry," Ariel said immediately.

"I can imagine, but I am kind of hungry. Ellie?"

Ellie nodded. "Yes, thank you."

"I'll be back in a few. Let's take a little break."

Ariel glanced after her when Jordan got up to leave, waiting until the door was closed before she turned back to Ellie.

"She's nice."

"Yeah, I think so, too," Ellie agreed. "Ariel—we'll do whatever we can to help, so if you need anything, please don't hesitate to ask."

"I don't mind talking to you, I really don't," Ariel said. "I don't ever want to go back. If I have to stay up all night, that's okay. I hate them so much."

Ellie laid a hand on her arm, carefully, but Ariel didn't seem to mind the light touch. She couldn't promise that it would all be okay to the girl who had lost her mother today, because it would never be completely okay...but they could try to help her make it through the worst of it. Beyond tonight, she feared, Ariel's future was uncertain.

CPS would find her an emergency placement and hopefully a permanent home soon, but with the cult's lawyers fighting back, she might have to testify in court.

Ariel had a long, difficult path ahead—and they still didn't know anything about Lilah Strickland's whereabouts.

⁂

Outside the door, Jordan would have liked a private moment to herself, but of course that wasn't possible. A woman from CPS was waiting with A.D.A. Esposito and an agent.

"Any word on Strickland yet?"

The agent shook her head. She didn't offer any other commentary.

"How soon can you wrap this up?" The CPS employee asked. "She's obviously exhausted. Since her father was among the arrests, and the mother...I have arranged a temporary home for her, and I think it would be for the best..."

"She hasn't eaten in a while," Jordan cut her off. "I'll get her dinner, and then we can finish for today. I need the address of the temporary home, so we can send an officer there. I imagine that we can't hold everyone here forever, and she's talking. Someone might take offense."

The truth was, if Ariel didn't want food, Jordan needed something badly. She had a blinding headache, and she wasn't even sure if a sandwich would cure it—it was worth a try. She wondered when Ariel was going to fall apart and wished fervently that an adult would be there for her in that moment.

"I'll make sure you have all the information."

"Thanks."

Jordan remembered her meetings with her former CI Darla Pierson, before Darla had a home and a baby of her own. Darla had enjoyed everything sweet. It wasn't the solution to everything, but it could be a tiny comfort on this complicated day—for everyone involved. She hurried to the bakery across the street and bought some bagels and pastries, specialty coffees for the adults and a juice for Ariel, hoping that would carry them all through the evening.

They were lucky to have a witness like Ariel who was clear and concise for her age, even if her determination was a surface that could crack at any moment, when she realized what lay ahead for her. In the best-case scenario, the father would go away for a long time, all of them would, though that made Ariel's future still unclear.

Living with her birthparents had been difficult for Jordan, and scary at times. Living without them had been difficult at first, too, and she hardly ever thought about the strange time in between, not knowing where she'd end up.

All of that was coming back to her now. While she hadn't been born into a culture of respect, Jim and Kathryn hadn't belonged to a women-hating cult that shut them off from the rest of the world. Deborah had wanted to leave, build a different future for her and Ariel.

Maybe Kathryn had similar hopes at some point, even though the only way she could realize them was to leave her own child with complete strangers better equipped to give her a home.

Maybe the CPS employee was right, and they needed to leave it here for today. With no news about Strickland, the workday was far from over.

❧

Ariel gave the woman from CPS a doubtful look, turning back to Jordan and Ellie.

"You're sure I don't have to go back to him?"

"Your dad is facing some serious charges," Jordan reminded her. "Ms. Lang here will make sure you're okay. She has arranged somewhere for you to stay for now. We'll have an officer in front of your house. I promise you it's safe."

"Are you sure? Dad is going to be so pissed...mad at me."

"He can't do anything to you."

"I can come with you," Ellie said. "I'll stay for a while, and I can call someone to take over for the night. How does that sound?"

The girl didn't quite manage a smile, but the corners of her mouth twitched with the surprise. "You would do that?"

"Of course. I'll be back later," she said to Jordan. "Can you keep one of those bagels for me?"

This time, she was rewarded with a small smile from Ariel before they left the department with Ms. Lang.

Jordan went back into the room to gather the remnants of their impromptu dinner, realizing the agent was still outside.

"Would you like one?" she asked, holding up the bag.

"Oh God, thank you so much." The woman helped herself to a donut, before Jordan locked the door. There were at least a dozen members of the cult still being interrogated, others waiting. The FBI would want their hands on the weapons dealers first, find out what they were planning with that arsenal, and who else was involved, but there were individuals with a long list of accusations against them that they would have to deal with.

Furthermore, they had to check the IDs of the women and children against the Missing Persons database, since not all of them had been born into the cult.

She had talked to a couple of women, then joined the interrogation of a man and his second wife who had both been complicit in "gifting" their daughter to Daniel Deane. Several times during those interviews Jordan wished she hadn't eaten anything, her stomach lurching. Then, bit by bit, the conversations came to a halt. They could tell who was relevant to the Prophets by the priorities their lawyers set. Just their presence seemed to upset the women who were here not because they were accused of anything, but as possible witnesses.

Jordan hated that they felt intimidated even here. They were doing their best to keep them away from their husbands' lawyers, but of course they couldn't stop the attorneys from talking to them, as only one of the women admitted she felt threatened.

"I hear you're giving out food, which is nice, but I'm still here too."

Bethany sat on the edge of her desk. "You're willing to share what's in that bag, I hope?"

Jordan leaned back in her chair, thinking she could probably get Ellie something else later.

"I hope you have good news," she said.

"We claimed all of our wackos and gladly leave you the rest."

"I figured."

"I see it looks less like a kindergarten and more like a police department again. I assume everyone is accounted for."

Jordan nodded. "It's...complicated," she said. "They were either born into the family or cut ties with their own a long time ago. They are so used to the men taking care of everything, they are completely overwhelmed. I had a couple of social workers talk to them."

"That's good. You're doing okay."

For some reason, Jordan thought the soft tone was inappropriate for work. Bethany had accepted the status quo, but that didn't mean they had the friendship-with-the-ex down pat yet.

"What about Strickland?"

"Oh God, this is a disaster. I have some colleagues on the case full time, and I'd be looking for her too if it wasn't for the other million things I need to do and explain to my boss whom I'm currently hiding from. We have one dead body, and we're missing an agent and a founding brother. Jeremiah Deane wasn't here or at the Iowa compound. This is going to cost me."

"It wasn't you fault."

Bethany shrugged. "Nobody cares, and frankly, if Lilah's okay, I can postpone my plans, no problem. Where's Harding?"

"Ariel wanted her to come with her. She'll get her settled in, and have another officer replace her later."

"Hm. Okay."

Jordan didn't quite know what to make out of that comment, and it worried her.

"What does that mean?"

"Nothing. You should go home and sleep for a few hours—at least you have the luxury while those lawyers keep stalling. I'll see you tomorrow if I still have a job by then."

"Okay. Good luck."

Jordan checked her phone, but there was no news from Ellie. She texted her to meet at the *D&T* in a couple of hours. Tonight, she wasn't going to sleep in the haunted house.

Chapter Thirteen

The woman who took in Ariel was in her fifties, an experienced and trusted foster mother. Ellie breathed a sigh of relief when she saw the house, the kitchen/dining/living area a light and open space. Mrs. Milner's bedroom was on the first floor, Ariel's upstairs.

As they walked up the stairs, Ellie could tell that Ariel was losing energy rapidly. The dreams she and her mother had shared had vanished into thin air. All of a sudden, she was by herself—which was probably the preferable alternative to being with her father, but still.

"The bathroom is stacked with everything you need, but if there's anything else, please, just ask," Mrs. Milner explained. "You might not be here for long, but I want you to be comfortable and know you're welcome."

Ariel mustered a small smile. "Thanks," she whispered.

The room, like the others, was light and welcoming, fairly gender neutral in décor. Ellie stepped into the adjacent bathroom and took a quick look around. Ariel was motivated. She wanted the people responsible for her mother's death be held accountable. She wanted to see that happen, so why would she harm herself? Better to be safe than sorry. Finding nothing that could be turned into a weapon without much creative use, she turned, seeing Mrs. Milner's thoughtful gaze.

"We have to think of everything, I know," the older woman said.

Ellie nodded. She went back to Ariel who stood in the middle of the room, looking lost.

"They didn't tell me if you had eaten, so I made dinner. It's ready whenever you are, and later I can show you the rest of the house. You can watch TV if you like...just take your time. There's no hurry."

"Sounds okay, right? We'll check in with you tomorrow, I promise."

There was a flash of panic on the girl's face. "What if they come here?"

"I don't think that's going to happen, but there'll be a cop outside the house all night."

"What if that's not enough?"

"You'll be safe here," Mrs. Milner said, and to Ellie, "I have experience with groups like this. I agree with you, I don't think they'll try anything tonight. If they did, we can handle them."

"Um...can I talk to Ellie for a moment?"

"Sure. I'll be downstairs if you need me."

When the two of them were alone, Ellie said, "Suddenly I think it was a bad idea to have bagels and donuts. I didn't know there would be dinner."

Ariel didn't react, just slumped on the bed.

"I know this is hard. I understand, but you're not alone."

"Because of the other girls? Most of them will want nothing to do with me, and the rest...they are too far gone."

Ellie suppressed a shudder. "This will make a difference for all of you. You can live your lives and be free now."

"But Mom won't."

Ellie hadn't seen it coming at all. The next moment, Ariel wrapped her arms around her, holding on tight, and the flood-gates finally opened. Ellie embraced her in return, her own throat tight, her eyes prickling with tears she couldn't cry right now.

"I know. I know it's not fair. I'm so sorry."

"She didn't want to leave me behind. If she had gone to meet the agents, she might still be alive."

"We don't know that." Ellie didn't say that in that case, the killer might have gotten to Ariel instead. It was a no-win situation, and they still had to build on that and make as many arrests as possible stick. Those men, once free, would continue the same way, start over somewhere else, because they believed it was their God-given right to have multiple teenage wives. The women and girls who had been living on the compound had a chance now—all of that would be gone if their husbands couldn't be convicted.

They needed Ariel to tell the truth and maybe encourage others to do so. Ellie hated to place that kind of burden on a child, but she couldn't think of any alternative.

"I wish I could just hide somewhere. I don't want to talk anymore, have them feel sorry for me, but...I'm scared."

"You and your mom were with some pretty scary people, but you never have to go back."

"But where will I go?"

"With someone nice like Mrs. Milner. For sure."

Ellie wanted to kick herself for making what might be a premature promise—but she'd do whatever it took to help Ariel through this first, worse moments.

Ariel wasn't ready to let go yet. Neither was Ellie.

"I know it's hard to see right now, but you will get through this."

"How do you know that?"

Ellie took a deep breath. And another. The words that had come together in her head easily, wouldn't come out now. She felt a tear tickling her face.

"My parents died in a car accident," she finally said. "I was older than you. It hurt. I still miss them, but I don't want to hide anymore. You'll get there too."

She wiped a hand across her face and slowly pulled back, reaching for the tissue box on the nightstand. She took one and held the box out to Ariel.

"You'll come back here tomorrow?"

"Yes. We'll have to talk to the Assistant District Attorney. I can't promise that you won't have to go to court...but maybe she'll just need your statement."

Ellie was aware that she might have promised too much already. Ariel seemed calmer now. If that's what it took, she was all right with it.

"That's okay," Ariel said with a sigh. "I'll be dead to them now that they know I talked to the police, which is...It doesn't matter. I want them to pay for what they did to Mom."

"And they will. Would you like to come down and get some dinner after all? If I remember correctly, my colleagues ate most of those donuts."

"Sure. She seems okay."

Ariel got up from the bed, then hesitated.

"Is there anything else, sweetie?"

The girl was shifting from one foot to the other before she asked, "Were you in the car? With your parents?"

"No. It took me some time, but eventually I was able to be grateful. I was given a second chance."

It was a lot to process for both of them. Ellie thought it was best for now to leave Ariel in Mrs. Milner's capable hands, hoping she had said the right things.

Bethany didn't go home, and neither did Jordan when she was asked to sit in on the interrogation of Ariel's father, Nathan, who owned the leather store.

"We might have a lead on Lilah," Bethany said. "Russo and another agent are on it, but I still want to have a chat with Nathan tonight. And I want another woman in there because I know it pisses them off."

"Wow, thanks. That makes me sound really qualified."

"Don't expect flattery at this time of day," Bethany returned. "I hear everything is settled for Ariel over at Mrs. Milner's."

Jordan hadn't spoken to Ellie since she'd left with Ariel.

"That's great to know."

"Yeah. Milner is a retired agent. There won't be any surprises."

With some vehemence, Bethany yanked the door to the room that held Nathan Deane, open. This particular family was at the heart of the case: Deborah Deane had apparently helped Jennifer Beaumont hide a copy of the book, then she befriended Lilah Strickland, meanwhile planning her escape from the Prophets for her and her daughter. Somebody found out and murdered her, and here was her husband Nathan, father to Ariel and husband to at least two "wives" besides Deborah which put him higher in the hierarchy than most. The youngest was sixteen now, mother to a one-year-old.

Jordan vowed to do whatever she could so that this man wouldn't go near his teenage daughter or any of the women he'd abused, ever again.

He frowned when they entered the room but didn't comment.

Bethany gave Jordan a triumphant look.

"It's funny how those things work in your family," she said to him. "If you don't piss off the brothers, you can be out on bail in a few hours. They could probably pay the lawyers for all of you, but they want to cut their losses. Which means...It's your right not to talk to us. You'll also get your ass thrown in jail."

"Watch that foul mouth of yours," he muttered.

"Oh, I don't know why I should. You like to tell women how to dress and when to talk, but we're not in your house anymore. This is *my* house. You don't have a say anymore. It's not fun, is it?"

"I'll be out of here sooner than you think. We'll sue all of you, the department, the FBI. You had no right to come in and tear our families apart."

"Wrong. The fact that you abuse young girls in that house of horrors gives me the right. And I haven't even started about buying guns from the black market. You might not want to go into details, but the guys who sold them to you will, I promise you that. You were preparing for Armageddon?"

"You don't understand a thing," he spat. "I wouldn't expect you to."

"What about your daughter, Ariel?" Jordan asked. "Do you really want this to be the memory she keeps of you?"

She didn't actually hope to appeal to his conscience. He had as little as her own biological father—but they needed to be clear on the facts and where to go from here.

"I don't care what the little bitch thinks," he said.

Jordan kept her expression careful neutral. Both she and Bethany had seen too much to be surprised, but it was still a blow.

"What? She's betraying every one of us, like her mother. They're the spawn of the devil. I only regret that it took me so long to realize that. I don't want to see her lying face ever again."

"Is that why you killed Deborah? You found out she'd been lying to you?"

"I didn't kill her, even though she surely wasn't worth much to me. She couldn't even give me a son, just that good-for-nothing girl. Then I realized she was hiding that filthy book Jennifer wrote. I wanted to discipline her, try to teach her, but not kill her. She still had to do her part in raising the children."

Yes, four children from three different "wives," one of them still underage.

The red tape would be a nightmare, Jordan thought. Illegal marriages, missing birth certificates. They needed the help of the other women. There was no way they could solely rely on a traumatized thirteen-year-old. Jordan felt relieved that Nathan seemed to have no intention of claiming his parental rights, but at the same time, his attitude was draining.

She wasn't sure whether he'd killed Deborah, but he certainly didn't mind harm coming to her or Ariel. It was hitting too close to home.

"Again, without your father's and uncles' lawyers, you might not get that far."

"I have the right to a public defender," he said, sounding unsure for the first time. "I want one now."

When Jordan finally made it out of the precinct, she had only minutes to spare until meeting Ellie. She considered meeting her at the apartment instead, when Bethany caught up with her in the parking lot.

"Hey, would you mind giving me a ride? I feel like drinking tonight."

"That's not a good idea. Tomorrow will be early."

"You're going, aren't you?"

"Just one—" Jordan stopped, reminding herself that she didn't need to share this kind of detail with Bethany. "All right."

"Thanks. I'll catch a cab later."

"Any news on Strickland?" Jordan asked after they'd sat in the car.

Bethany shrugged, leaning back in her seat with a sigh. "We are working with someone who might have seen her. Russo is still following up on that. We still don't know why she wasn't at the compound today, or who she's with now. Some people are starting to raise questions, and either way, it doesn't look good for me. I'm saying that because it's true, not because I'm a selfish bitch. Either something happened to her, or she did something...I know I didn't make a bad judgment call. She's capable, and she didn't turn on us."

"It's not your fault. These things can get out of control quickly."

"You don't have to tell me that."

They drove the rest of the way in silence. When they arrived, Bethany asked, "Do you want me to wait?"

"Don't be ridiculous. Come on."

Ellie sat at a table with Kate and Derek, waving to her. Bethany didn't follow her but stayed at the bar instead. When Jordan got to the table, Ellie stood and embraced her, and a bit of the day's exhaustion fell away.

"Hey. That's a nice greeting."

"Yeah." Ellie sighed. "I needed nice. Since you're almost in time, I forgive you for bringing your ex. No, that didn't come out right. I don't care. Wow. What a day."

"It was." Jordan pulled herself a chair, and, when the waitress came by, ordered a Corona.

"What's this?" Derek asked. "You're driving her around now?"

Her partner, as it turned out, was less forgiving when it came to Bethany, still.

"Give it a rest. She asked for a ride. We were going to the same place."

164

"I don't like the way you keep indulging her."

"And I don't think this is appropriate."

"I agree," Ellie said. "I get to judge that."

Derek Henderson shook his head, exasperated. "She wants to advance her career, just like that other time, and once again, someone gets hurt. She never faces any consequences."

Jordan didn't feel like having this conversation, now, or ever. She particularly didn't like that Derek put her in a position where she felt like she had to defend Bethany in front of Ellie. Fortunately, Ellie knew her enough to understand her struggle.

"I think we were all angry with her back then, and I understand that there was some sort of protocol. I hope that you'd say the same things if she was a guy, and besides, Jordan doesn't want to talk about it. That should be enough."

"Thank you. I love you."

"Whatever," Derek scoffed. "You got out while you could, that's great, but she could still drag you down with her career-wise. And those women? They are all terrified. One or two might talk, but if she keeps pushing them, it will come at a cost. You know that."

"Derek," Kate said softly.

"I'm done," he said, holding up his hands in defeat. "Don't say I didn't warn you."

"All right, I get it."

An awkward silence settled between them for long moments, before Kate said, "I know we're not supposed to talk about the case anymore but I, for one, am glad we finally get to figure out why Jennifer was killed. I'm sure her mother will be grateful once it's not in the headlines every day anymore. And we are helping those women. We did. Some might be confused right now, but every single one is better off than she was yesterday."

To Jordan's relief, Derek simply agreed.

"For sure. I'm afraid this case will make headlines for some time to come. You'd like another one?" he asked with regard to Kate's empty glass.

"Yes, please."

He got up, and after exchanging a look with Ellie, Jordan followed him.

"Are you all right?"

"Are you?" he asked and shrugged. "Look, I'm sorry. I assume you know what you're doing."

Derek ordered a couple of beers and went back to their table. Jordan regarded the price list written on the chalkboard behind the back.

"Everything on that sounds good right now," Bethany said behind her.

"Sorry. I'm not paying."

"Don't worry, I'm good. You know what this is all about, right?" Bethany took a seat on a barstool.

"What do you mean?" Jordan asked, before she even realized she didn't want to have this conversation. Maybe Derek had a point. Some of those dynamics were still familiar between then.

"I know I failed you. I dealt with it. I don't think your partner has. He couldn't save you, and he still blames himself."

"That's an awful lot of psychoanalysis for tonight. Besides, I thought you were moving away, so you won't have to deal with any of it for much longer."

Jordan had been right, and she should have known better. With Bethany, it was never just small talk.

"I won't go anywhere if this blows up in my face, pardon the bad pun. I need this to work out, and I need Lilah to be all right."

"I hope she is. Good luck." Jordan had been about to get a cocktail for Ellie, but she decided that with a couple on beers, she'd be out of here sooner.

"You will forgive me? Eventually?"

"Oh, come on. Go home, sleep. I'll see you tomorrow."

"Yeah."

Not inclined to indulge Bethany's moodiness any longer, Jordan picked up her order and went back to Ellie, realizing Derek and Kate were gone.

"I guess it's just me," Ellie said wistfully.

Jordan leaned over to kiss her before she sat down. "That's perfect."

Never mind what was up with Bethany or Derek tonight.

⸎

"I suppose you don't want to talk any more about the case either," Ellie assumed, testing the waters. She knew that in some form she'd have to. She felt herself unable to shake off what she and Ariel had shared in that conversation, and she was unsure whether she had found the right words with the grieving teen, or if her own grief was making itself known, still lingering.

She hadn't lied, though. She had taken life head on, pursued every opportunity. Her belief in this approach had only grown stronger after she'd been attacked on her way home. She wasn't going to let a woman-hating lowlife determine the way she lived her life—or a drunk driver.

"It's okay. How did it go with Ariel?"

"Okay. She's scared, but she will help us any way she can. I think she'll do fine if she has to go to court. She's just worried that they might try to come for her. There's no chance, right?"

"Not from the father anyway." Jordan sighed. "What a creep. I mean...it's better for her that he doesn't want her, but at the same kind, it's...cold."

"Wow." Ellie thought of the smart, brave girl who was ready to take on the Prophets even if no one else did. This man certainly didn't deserve her. Jordan's biological father wasn't cut from better cloth. Ariel brought up some uncomfortable truths for both of them. Deborah Deane had tried, but she wouldn't be able to enjoy the freedom she'd wanted for their daughter. "I hope she'll be surrounded by the right people now. That can make all the difference in the world. It's a terrible loss."

Jordan's gaze on her told Ellie that she was reading between the lines.

"Yeah, it made me think of my parents. I wasn't that young, and it was still hard...for a while, just to keep going, get out of bed every day."

"I'm sorry," Jordan said softly.

"Thank you. I told her we'd check in with her tomorrow."

"That's good. We're asking a lot of her. She should know that we will protect her."

"True."

At the end of this day, with its mixed emotions, Ellie felt confident and happy in the fact that they were together—never mind the sometimes awkward work situation with Bethany around, the horrors they were confronted with, or their own personal struggles. Being together. It made more sense than anything.

Kate and Derek were not at the apartment. Ellie took it as a good sign, even though this was one of the rare moments the roommate situation frustrated her. Tonight, she wanted affirmation, clothes all over the floor, reckless and passionate love-making—as it was, she still had to restrain herself somewhat, so her roommate wouldn't walk in on them.

Fortunately, Jordan understood her without so many words once they'd closed the door of Ellie's bedroom. Ellie hadn't had time to make the bed earlier this morning. It didn't matter.

The next time she caught a glimpse at the clock on the night-stand, it was nearly an hour after their arrival. Lying on her stomach, she sighed in pleasure as Jordan traced a finger down her spine. She hadn't been this truly relaxed in a while.

"Thank you," she whispered. "I really needed that."

Jordan laughed. "It wasn't entirely un-selfish." It might have been the sexy, sated tone to her voice, or her gentle touch that sent a shiver skittering down Ellie's spine. "We should get some sleep now."

"I guess you're right." She moved a little, fitting herself into Jordan's embrace. Jordan was right. If there were subjects they still needed to discuss, now was certainly not the best time to bring them up. Ellie didn't know if she'd be brave enough so soon again.

"Move in with me," she said. "I mean it."

Jordan was silent, probably wondering if she'd heard her correctly.

"I know you're hesitating, and yes, a lot of things could go wrong. But it could also be all right this time, and why wouldn't it be? We already tried. We're basically living together anyway, just with an annoying commute that we could get rid of. Please, don't say no before you hear me out."

"I wasn't going to say no, but I can still hear you out," Jordan said.

Ellie turned to look at her incredulously. "What? I mean, that's great," she hastened to add. "We both had difficult experiences living with other people, but this is different. It's about us."

"I've been thinking about it," Jordan admitted. "The house...I liked it from the moment I first saw it, but that was a different situation. I know you don't care much for it, and when we do this, I want you to be comfortable. I needed to buy it, and I needed to stay there after..." She didn't finish the sentence.

Ellie didn't need an explanation. It had been hard for her when Bethany took over right there at the scene, when things between them had been up in the air for a while.

"I understand. And I know I promised to give you time. I'm going to keep that promise. I just want you to know I'm ready."

Instead of an answer, Jordan pulled her close again. For a moment, Ellie was worried about what that could mean, until Jordan said, "I'll have to look for a new realtor sometime soon, then."

"I love you so much."

There were many things they couldn't control, like who their parents were, or what happened to them along the way—their living situation was not one of those things. The new possibilities made her excited about the future. Ellie was still nowhere near able to sleep.

Chapter Fourteen

K ate had never come home that night, and she was late at roll call, looking tired.

"Don't ask," she murmured as she slid onto the chair next to Ellie.

"I wasn't going to."

Ellie was tired, too, but she was also still on a high from last night's conversations and otherwise communication.

Sergeant Bristol was about to speak when the door opened again, and Bethany walked in, still wearing her coat. Apparently, she'd just arrived as well. Jordan hadn't told her that much, but Ellie assumed that with Strickland missing, she was in hot water with her supervisors. She couldn't say she felt any good about it. Whatever her personal issues with her might be, she wasn't looking for her to fail. If you believed Henderson, she kept bringing that on herself, but Ellie wasn't sure if that was the whole truth.

She cast a sideways glance at Kate, reminded that she would have to have a talk with her. Ellie had made a promise to her too, that she wouldn't leave her hanging with the rent the way Rhonda had done it to her. She was already starting to have a guilty conscience. In any case, it would only be a first heads-up—Jordan would have to go through quite a bit of paperwork in order to get rid of the house. They hadn't made any decision as to where they would live together, or whether to rent or buy.

Then, there was the detective's exam coming up.

"Officer Harding?" Startled, with all eyes on her, Ellie realized that Sergeant Bristol probably hadn't said her name for the first time. "Dr. Roberts would like you to accompany her today."

Kate raised her eyebrows, and Ellie shrugged at her. She had no idea what this could mean, but she hoped she was going to learn Lilah Strickland was safe. She hurried to get up and follow Bethany outside of the room.

"You heard from Lilah?"

"Sort of," Bethany said. "Come on, there's not a lot of time."

"Time for what?"

"To brief you on your assignment. Frankly, I wish we had some better alternatives, but you know this case. You know the people involved, and there's no way we can pull anyone away from this investigation right now, so, congrats."

"Thanks...I guess."

"You will be grateful. I promise you, it will look good on your résumé."

They walked along the corridor and to the elevator, where Bethany pressed the button for the lobby. Ellie was surprised to find they were leaving the building, walking a few steps towards a dark van. Bethany knocked on the side door.

A man wearing the FBI jacket opened it to them. He cast a dubious look at Ellie.

"She was there during the arrests?"

"Yes, but the brothers don't know her. Lilah does. It's just going to be a distraction, a quick in and out."

"If you say so."

Ellie saw another man, wearing plain clothes, and then, with a start, she realized that she'd seen him before.

He noticed her reaction and, with a friendly smile, extended his hand. "I see you remember me from the bar. I'm Joseph. I came to the conclusion it was better to be on the right side of the law, and I'm glad I could do it early enough to help. Lilly—I mean Lilah—is holding on, but she is in grave danger."

Ellie felt like she'd been transported into an alternate universe. What had happened to her day job? Moving in together with Jordan?

"What can I do?" she asked, her question meant for Bethany and the other agent.

"You know that this was a joined operation with the precincts and FBI field offices in Arizona and Iowa. We were able to deal a substantial blow to the cult, but Jeremiah Deane got away. He was supposed to be present that day, but no one can find him."

"He was tipped off?"

"Maybe. In any case, he and some loyal followers have holed up in a secure location, and they took some of the women with them."

"You mean not everyone in the compound was accounted for?"

Bethany's expression was somber. "We are still trying to figure that out, but these people don't exactly put a lot of trust in our government. They haven't filled out all the paperwork, birth certificates, marriage licenses, and they've done this for many years. Add to that some missing women that were 'taken in' by them. Were they kidnapped or did they join freely? It's still a hot mess. So yes, we assume that they took some of them. Lilah was able to give us a location, but we need someone to ring the doorbell while we take the place down."

"I'll be what, the pizza delivery girl?"

"No. Lilah's sister."

"I don't understand," Ellie said honestly.

"I guess this is where I come in," Joseph said, sporting the same cordial smile. "The problem you had before was that Raphael was giving you only part of the information. I decided to work with the authorities, because I didn't like the way they treated the women there. I know everything that's going on."

"That means Ariel might not even have to testify?"

"She was going to?" he asked. "I thought she was quite young to face such a challenge. I'm truly willing to help where I can...and I'm going to introduce you to Jeremiah. They will let us in, because unlike Raphael, I'm not persona non grata. You can check on Lilah, see what she needs. At this point, we know she contacted one of your agents, but what we don't know is if she went with them freely."

"So we know for sure she's still alive?"

"I'm glad to be able to confirm that," Joseph said. "I'm honored that the FBI trusts me enough to let me help them. It's a terrifying situation on the inside, and it has to end."

Behind his back, Ellie saw Bethany roll her eyes which said clearly that her willingness to work with someone from the family had more to do with a desperate situation than with trust.

"I'm in. So what location are we talking about?" she asked.

Bethany smiled. "Not too far. Just a short helicopter ride. And no, you can't call Jordan. She's going to be mad at me as it is, but I believe in asking forgiveness rather than permission. Let's go," she said to the driver.

A tired Casey Lyons informed Jordan that everything had been silent overnight at Mrs. Milner's house. Ariel was holding up, and none of the cult members had tried to make contact. That was at least good news.

Ellie wasn't at the department, probably in a squad car right now, and Bethany was M.I.A. Jordan went down the lab to talk to the medical examiner about Deborah Deane, hoping she could give her something that would point them to the killer.

For Ariel's sake, and frankly, her own, she hoped they wouldn't find out it was Nathan who had killed his own wife. His emotions for her seemed to be more in the range of indifference.

They still had to figure out if the men and women they'd encountered yesterday were really all that lived on the compound, and if that number had changed, why. Jennifer had left, Deborah had wanted to, and they were both dead. They had found Eileen Yates. Otherwise, they had yet to match any other of the cold cases, women who had gone missing all those years ago.

She saw Valerie Esposito leave her office and got up as well.

"Hey," Valerie said. "I see you're buried in paperwork just as I am. This case is a nightmare of red tape, but I believe we're making progress. The rest will be up to the federal prosecutors. I was going to see the girl, Ariel."

"Do you mind if I come with you?"

"Trying to escape that paperwork, aren't you?"

"Ellie was with her yesterday. We promised to check up on her."

"Sure. It's a shame about the mother, but I'm glad we got her out. I think she's our best bet, unless Roberts can come through with her mystery witness—and I believe it when I see it."

"Mystery witness?" Jordan asked, surprised.

"So, she didn't tell you the whole story. I am not surprised."

Jordan chose not to answer. The day had started on a too perfect note to get involved in another argument about Bethany. She was still amazed at how easy it had been in the end, to actually say it, yes, she was on board with all of Ellie's plans.

All this time she'd been reluctant, hesitant, but she had to go with the evidence. They were good together, and too smart to recreate old patterns. As for the man who had sold her the house and now served a lifelong prison sentence—she was cutting the last tie. In the next few days, she would tackle the task of finding a new realtor.

"I hate giving her credit, but Roberts and her people did some good work on this," Valerie said. "It's near miraculous that we'll finally be able to shut them down, but it looks good. I conferred with my colleagues in Arizona and Iowa, and they're pretty thrilled, except for one thing. Jeremiah was supposed to be there for the gun sale."

"I heard. That's odd indeed. What was that you said about the mystery witness?"

Valerie shrugged. "I'll know when you know, I guess. Roberts is still working out the finer details with him, and it's all very recent as I understand."

"She said anything about Strickland? You talked to her today?"

"No, not since last night. Okay, let's do this."

They had arrived at the house.

Mrs. Milner opened the door to them, looking somber.

"I get her to eat meals," she said, "but she's not opening up much—other than the bare, ugly facts anyway."

"We'll be as careful as we can," Valerie assured her.

"I hope you'll be. You can stay in the kitchen. I'll be in my office. Ariel," she called. "The lady from the DA's office is here to see you."

Ariel sat at the kitchen table, morosely staring into her glass of orange juice. However, her face lit up when she saw Jordan. "I didn't know you were coming. Is Ellie here, too?"

Jordan was aware of Valerie's bemused gaze. She hadn't expected this kind of welcome either.

"No. She's really busy at the moment, but she'll come by later. I wanted to see how you're doing?"

"Like it's all a bad dream, though I know it's not." She swallowed hard. "Did you find who killed my mom?"

"No, not yet, but we're close. For now, A.D.A. Esposito will have to ask you some more questions."

"Do I have to go to court? Ellie said there might be a chance I won't have to."

"Well, I'm afraid Ellie doesn't decide these things, but there is indeed a chance. We want to prepare for all possibilities though, and I need to hear the whole story from you."

Ariel gave her a look that was much too grown up for a thirteen-year-old.

"How much time do you have?"

Joseph was excited like never before in his life. He'd lived most of it under the radar, now, all of a sudden, he had become important to so many people: Jeremiah. Lilly. The lady from the FBI, and the new girl, an officer named Ellie who was going to pose as Lilly's sister, in order to take down the last of the cult.

The fact that Deborah and Nathan's daughter was helping the authorities complicated matters slightly. He didn't want to lose his position to a teenager, not when he was so close to realizing all his plans.

As it was, he still had a few aces up his sleeve. Ariel hadn't seen Deborah's murderer—he had.

The story could still go many ways, but he had a bargaining chip with the FBI...Now he had one with Jeremiah too.

Ellie was beyond nervous, and the helicopter ride was only a small part of it. Derek Henderson's warnings rang clearly in her head—Bethany would do whatever it took to advance her career and use whoever she wanted to. At least, that was one side of the story. She was also a woman trying to get ahead in a still male-dominated field, and, as far as Ellie could tell, she was dedicated. Dedicated to her job, to ending a woman-hating operation that had been going on for decades. She took risks. Ellie could relate to that. Defending Jordan's ex in her mind felt strange to her, but at least it was some sort of distraction.

If Bethany trusted Joseph, she should too, right? He would try to contact Jeremiah, make him give up the exact location where the remaining members of the Prophets were hiding out. They had to have driven all night to get anywhere near this area.

Ellie had listened closely in the briefing, and she knew what she had to do, and what she was getting herself into. In fact, Bethany was right. This was a chance to prove herself even before the exam, and she'd do her best. She also remembered taking cover behind the shed with Casey, bullets flying. The women who had lost their lives because of the cult, and those who were still unable to escape its tight grip even though they were technically free.

They could only hope that Jeremiah Deane and his people hadn't made Lilah yet, and even then, it would not be easy to get her out. Ellie had to be eyes and ears for the team waiting outside.

A car was waiting for them, taking them to a hotel room where the command center was set up.

"Remember," Bethany said, "no going off script. Joseph is going to do most of the talking. You figure out where Lilah is, and what's her condition. We do the rest."

"I understand."

"Good. Now let's have Joseph talk to Jeremiah, and we'll go from there."

Everyone waited in tense silence as Joseph made the call. He had insisted Jeremiah would answer if he heard from him—and the founder of the Prophets of Better Days did.

"Brother Jeremiah, it's Joseph. I need to talk to you," he said. "Yes, I know. It's awful, but I think the lawyers are doing an amazing job. I hear Daniel will be out on bail tomorrow at the latest."

Ellie cast a look at Bethany who shrugged. Joseph seemed to sell the bold-faced lie quite well, and that's all that counted. After being caught red-handed with a carload of illegal weapons, bail for the leader of the local compound was very much uncertain.

"Yes, that's good news. He might have to lay low for a while, but that's okay. I can pass on whatever you need, but...that's not why I called you. It's about Lilly." He listened for a while. "I know she wants to stay with us. I met Lilly's sister, and she hopes to see her for a few minutes. Yes, I know we don't do that, but this is different. If we let her talk to Lilly and convince her that she's okay, she'll walk away. Otherwise...I don't know—no, not that I know of. I believe we can trust her. I'm aware. She's not like Jennifer. Daniel made a lot of mistakes, but we can do better. I promise you. Okay, I'll tell her."

Abruptly, the phone call ended.

"What?" Bethany asked tersely. "Do you have the location?"

"Not yet."

"What the—you told us you were certain he'd tell you!"

"And he will," Joseph said, his tone calm and matter-of-fact. "I had to be careful. We all know what's going to happen if he suspects something. They're going to greet us with gunfire. It's tricky as it is, but I think he understands the only way to stay under the radar is to let her in. I don't think they know Lilly is with the FBI. If they think Ellie is the only family member looking for her, they'll want to see her, and take it from there."

"How do you even know they're anywhere near?" Ellie could understand Bethany's frustration with his attitude, but they needed him.

"Believe me, when you grow up with these people, you learn to read them. The brothers have lots of property in the area, and not even I know all of it. You already know that they're not too fond of the government and paperwork, so it's a too wide area, and you wouldn't find records of all of it anyway. Whatever they do, the brothers will always come out unscathed, because they have their scapegoats, like Raphael. They will rebuild unless we stop them."

"What do we do now?"

"We wait," Joseph said cheerfully. "Jeremiah will talk this over with whoever's with him and get back to me. Let him come to us. He's always fondest of taking in women from the outside and 'guiding' them."

Ellie's stomach lurched at that.

Chapter Fifteen

J ordan was once more in awe of the girl's incredible strength.
   While she could relate to growing up in an unsafe environment, she'd never faced the threats that had been everyday reality
for Ariel.

The brothers and their sons had the right to discipline children at any time, for any reason. They had, like the grown
women, to follow a strict behavioral code, and then there was
always the dreaded idea of marriage hanging over their heads.

Ariel confirmed that she had seen young women show up one
day, stay with them for a while and then disappear. When she
asked questions, her mother had warned her. It wasn't until a
few weeks ago that she had entrusted her with her decision to
leave. Deborah had stressed that she couldn't tell anyone, not
even her friends, not even Nathan's other wives who were barely
older than Ariel.

The case against the men they had arrested was airtight.
The guns, the systematic abuse of women and children, they
wouldn't get out of that so easily. The department psychiatrist,
Dr. Burns, had been talking to some of them, and the conversations continued. She would be able to testify that many of
them were traumatized. Sadly, most of them insisted that their
husbands were innocent.

There was still no sight of Ellie, but Jordan assumed she'd see her later tonight. Maybe they could celebrate—continue to celebrate—their decision. Not that it was going to happen overnight. If she wanted to get a good price for the house, she'd still have to invest a little, and, of course, find that realtor.

It seemed like a lifetime ago that she'd walked into Darby's agency, not knowing she was sitting down with a murderer to discuss her future living arrangements. She'd been off her game, too distracted with whatever else had been going on in her life, but perhaps that wasn't enough of an explanation. His cover had been damn good.

When she made time for a coffee between the continued paperwork and checked her phone, she found a text message from Kathryn.

"I am so grateful to have you in my life again. Thank you."

Jordan sighed. They were establishing the guidelines of their new relationship, and she was well aware she had to remain cautious. She was about to get back to her work when the lieutenant came hasting into the room.

"Carpenter, my office."

"Yes, sir."

She followed him, wondering if this had anything to do with Bethany or the fact that she hadn't checked in at all today. For some reason, everyone seemed to think that Jordan could be of help when it came to her.

To her surprise, Derek and Maria Doss joined them a moment later.

"Henderson, Carpenter, I need you to go to the Men's Correctional Center. Raphael Deane was found dead in his cell. Doss, you handle the communication with the FBI and the family's lawyers."

"I'm on it," she said, obviously glad to leave.

"Dr. Roberts isn't back?" Jordan asked, surprised, even as she was still taking in the news. Derek gave her a look she vaguely interpreted her as "told you so."

"Dr. Roberts is not in the building, but Agent Russo will catch up with you. For now, this is our jurisdiction."

"All right. Let's find out what happened."

Derek didn't object to her driving. Jordan could tell that he had something on his mind.

"Whatever you want to say, say it. I'm not happy with this either. It's...odd."

"I don't think you want to hear this."

"I'm not going to defend her, I swear. Esposito hinted that there was another possible witness, someone they're shielding for now. This is getting murkier by the minute."

"Tell me about it," he said. "Kate told me Roberts pulled Ellie out of roll call this morning. She didn't know what it was about, but with Strickland still missing, I think we can guess."

"Damn it!"

"Yeah, that's what I was thinking."

"No, I mean..." Jordan shook her head. "Bethany. I swear, I don't understand her. I...I don't even know what to say to this. Ellie has been working on this case pretty much from the beginning, and she deserves some credit, but this is—"

"Reckless?" Derek finished her sentence. "I agree. But I'll bet you she has an explanation."

"She better. I can't believe this."

The problem was, she knew what Ellie would say, and Bethany was probably well aware of the dynamics at play. She didn't want to interfere with Ellie's career in any way because she was worried—they had made that clear between them. However, she could have an opinion on Bethany's actions, and she didn't like them.

"Well, whatever it is, she'll check in eventually," Derek said. "And she always gets lucky in those situations."

"No. I can't even think about this right now."

They had a job to do, so did the FBI, so did Ellie. Jordan couldn't let herself get distracted by the thought that Ellie's fate depended on luck rather than skills, Bethany's and hers. She'd have that talk with Bethany later.

❧

"We found him like this, called the police right away. I touched his neck to check for a pulse, but of course there was none."

Jordan could easily tell how the guard had come to this assessment. The front of Raphael Deane's prison suit was drenched in blood.

She took a closer look, seeing that the suit was torn open at least an inch and a half. She winced at the thought that someone had managed to get an object with a blade this wide on the inside.

"Any witnesses?"

"You might want to talk to Eddie Peck. He shared a cell with him but wasn't there when it happened. Most inmates were in the courtyard, but a couple might have heard something. You can see them right now."

"We would appreciate that, thank you. Give us a moment, please?"

"Of course."

It was a tight space for her, Derek, and the medical examiner. Jonathan Darby would spend the rest of his days in a space like this, and so would her biological father for being responsible for the cold-blooded murder of a cop. They both knew who they had to thank for that.

She suppressed a shudder, taking a closer look.

"Multiple stab wounds," the ME explained. "He was still warm when they found him."

"Somebody was angry at him."

Jordan couldn't imagine that the cult members, some of them in custody, a few of them on the run, had a way of realizing a plan like this. Or had they planned for this all along? Paid someone?

She left the cell to find the guard who had waited a few steps away from the door.

"We are going to speak to any possible witnesses in a second. I need to know who else works on this floor, and who came to visit Raphael recently."

"I can tell you that," the guard said stiffly. "Since he was transferred here, no one ever came to visit him except the public defender. Kid always seemed terrified, so I don't think you'll find anything there. Deane kept under the radar. Most of my colleagues were either watching the yard, or in another wing. I told you, we already found you the ones who most likely saw something, if anyone did at all."

"Yes, that was quick, thank you. Are you aware of any fights Deane might have gotten into? Groups he ran with?"

"Lady...Detective," he corrected himself quickly. "I'm sorry. Deane was one of the most unspectacular inmates I've ever met. See what Peck and the two others have to say."

"We will, thanks," Derek said.

As they walked down the long corridors where the inmates were now under lockdown, Jordan remembered something she had successfully suppressed until now. Darby was behind one of those doors. Still blaming her, still fantasizing about her.

It was about time she got rid of the house and moved on with her life, but first they had to finish up these interviews—while Ellie was doing God knows what for Bethany.

The call came two hours later. Ellie already had regrets about having agreed to this assignment in the first place. Bethany wasn't her supervisor. If Sergeant Bristol was so happy about the turn of events was yet to be determined—he had already reminded her in no uncertain terms, not too long ago, of her role in the department. There was still a gap between where she was, and where she wanted to be, but Bethany didn't seem to mind.

Most of all, she was uncomfortable with the awkward atmosphere in the room, something that seemed to have little to do with the high profile of this case. A lot was on the line for everyone in this room—and Lilah Strickland whose cover could be blown any moment.

Joseph maintained the same calm and optimistic attitude, and maybe he had to, maybe it was the only thing to keep him sane after spending most of his life in an insane environment.

"Thank you so much, Jeremiah," he finally said. "I truly believe this is the right thing to do. She will understand the virtue of our way of life. She has to hear it from Lilly herself that the press and the cops are all lying. Yes, she's here right now. Okay."

In an unexpected turn of events, he held the phone out to Ellie.

Bethany nodded, and so she took it.

"Hello?" she said.

"I understand you are Lilly's sister."

"That's true. I've been hearing a lot in the news lately, and I am worried about her. I want to talk to her."

"How did you meet Joseph?"

For long, excruciating seconds, Ellie's mind was blank, then she answered, proud to keep her voice level. "I'm a clerk at the courthouse, and I approached him. I don't know if what the people are saying about you is true. All I want is to see for myself if Lilly is safe with you. If you can't do that, I might have to go to the police after all."

That earned her laughter from Jeremiah.

"And tell them what, young lady? That you spoke to me on the phone? That's not going to do anything. I am aware though, that many lies have been told about us recently. I invite you to come visit for a few days and talk to Lilly. You'll see that she is doing great."

"I would appreciate that," Ellie said, taking a deep breath. "I just want her to be okay."

"Give the phone to Joseph, and we'll arrange the details."

She did as she'd been told, and Joseph finished the call within a minute, this time with directions from Jeremiah.

"Well done," Bethany said.

Ellie didn't feel much relieved. The hardest part was yet to come.

Chapter Sixteen

T he director had set up a room where Jordan and Derek could talk to Raphael Deane's cell mate. Eddie Peck was serving a sentence for manslaughter.

"I can't tell you much about Deane," he said, "but I can tell you I'm seriously freaked out that someone came into the cell with a knife. You hear about this stuff, but you hope it never happens to you. If you keep your head down, you just might be fine. Man, that's bad."

"You're right," Jordan said. "That's why we want to clear this up as soon as possible. Did Raphael ever talk to you about his family, or why he was in prison?"

Eddie Peck shook his head. "Barely. He did pray a lot, and I know he was mad because the family didn't send their attorneys. He wasn't much of a talker."

Raphael Deane had found many words when it came to telling women how to dress, Jordan thought. But that wasn't a reason to kill anybody. Did he know more than he had told them? It was likely.

"Let's talk about today. Did you notice anything? Did he act differently?"

He gave her a shrug in answer. "Not that I know of. I saw him come out to the yard with the rest of us, and not much later, they called the lockdown. I didn't see anything."

There was a knock on the door, and the guard they had talked to earlier, Biggs, walked inside. "Detective? There's something you should see."

"Thank you. We're done here. Mr. Peck, if you remember anything else…"

"Yeah, I know. I'll tell them to call you, but don't hold your breath. There was nothing much to remember about him."

"All right. Thanks." Outside the door, Biggs told her, "We found the knife hidden in one of the bathrooms. Someone rinsed it before they hid it in the toilet tank, but there were still some bloodstains in the sink."

"I need to take a look."

"Of course."

A moment later she stepped into the restroom, thinking they should be so lucky to find prints on the knife, because trying to come up with any conclusive prints from the area around the toilet in question and the sink would be impossible. She'd have the crew go over it anyway, but she didn't have much hope.

"You'll want this too."

Biggs held up the knife in a plastic bag, making her wonder if he'd carried it with him the whole time.

Someone had washed off the blood, but the size of the blade definitely fit.

"It's a shame," the guard said. "We work around the clock, so this doesn't happen, but it still does. I don't know how it got in. Someone's been biding their time…I can vouch for all of my colleagues."

"I'm sure they appreciate it. We still have to talk to them."

"I understand. I'll let everyone know."

In the meantime, she called Maria Doss and learned that Daniel Deane hadn't been much saddened by his son's death.

"He said, and I quote, 'he could never follow the rules, so that doesn't surprise me.' That's kind of cold—and what's more, I think they must have orchestrated this somehow."

"How, when they're on the run? I'm not sure about this," Jordan admitted. "There is almost no way for an inmate to get this kind of knife on the inside. I mean...it's not something you can get through the scanner or smuggle in inside your body."

"Ugh."

"Yeah, my thoughts exactly."

"You think one of the guards helped the killer?"

"We have no proof of that whatsoever, but we're going to talk to them, see if there could be any loophole in the security process."

No matter how Raphael Deane's killer had gotten their hands on the weapon, it was a scary thought that they had managed in the first place. If they did, someone else might too.

Ellie was aware of the occasional sideways glances Joseph threw her, and she was unnerved by them.

He looked ahead with a mild smile on his face.

"I assumed you'd have many questions for me. Law enforcement has tried to get an opening for a long time."

"Many of our questions have already been answered. This is why two of the brothers have been arrested along with many more followers."

"True...but I don't think you really understand how deep those ideas run, and what they are willing to do for them."

What did he want, praise for his actions? Ellie wanted to get through the day, without getting shot at again, without anyone getting hurt.

"I'm sure Dr. Roberts told you she's grateful you're working with us, saving the lives of women and children."

"It's not easy for the boys either. Everything and everyone on this inside is their property."

"Then you must be relieved all of this is coming to an end."

"Oh yes. You have no idea."

"I suppose you're right."

"You're still doubting me?"

Ellie shook her head, and he smiled again.

"I knew it."

"It doesn't matter what I think. If we get out of there with Lilah, that's what matters."

He was silent for a moment, before he spoke again. "She's a remarkable young woman. She fooled all of us—well, I figured it out at some point, but the brothers are usually paranoid. She charmed them."

Ellie didn't think she had to answer to that. Eyes on the prize.

"Don't worry. I'm sure you can too. I can see that potential in you."

"Thanks," she muttered, gripping the steering wheel tighter as they left the street to change onto a dirt road.

They weren't far.

Back at the precinct, Jordan refrained from sending a worried text message to Ellie, and an angry one to Bethany, just barely. She had organized her notes—nothing new from the guards, no one had any idea how Raphael had ended up dead in his cell. No prints on the knife. As she'd predicted, the area around the sink where it was found was too contaminated to give them any meaningful results.

She remembered what Valerie had said about the mystery witness, wondering if there was a connection. Did they have something to offer to Raphael? Even if that were true, how would the family have found out—and the main question remained, how could they have pulled off the murder?

Biggs had been as helpful as he possibly could, but they didn't have much to go on.

You'll forgive me eventually? Promise?

"Oh no," she said out loud as Bethany's words came back to her, earning a quizzical look from Derek who sat at his own desk. That's what Bethany had meant, forgive her not for something in the past, but because she was going to involve Ellie in her strategy.

She called Bethany's cell phone, and to her surprise, Bethany picked up right away.

"Jordan, I'm a little busy here. Not now."

"Raphael Deane was murdered a few hours ago in his cell. No witnesses, no suspects as for now."

"Well, you'll figure it out. I need to go."

"Who is your mystery witness?" *And where is Ellie?*

"One has nothing to do with the other. I know you're pissed—"

"Jesus, Bethany."

"I'll have to let you go. I'll talk to you when I can."

Jordan shook her head at the phone and tossed it back onto her desk.

"I hate to say it, but I owe you a drink or two."

Derek chuckled. "I do like the sound of that."

If only Ellie returned from this assignment to tell her all her worries had been unfounded. Jordan struggled to focus her attention on Biggs' statement—and then something jumped to mind.

As they walked up to the log cabin-style house, Ellie had to resist the impulse to look behind her. She was certain someone was watching them, and not just the agents that had parked their vehicle in a safe distance.

Joseph approached the house with a brisk step, and she had to hurry to keep up. The cordial smile was replaced by an unreadable expression. The remaining members of the Prophets of Better Days cult had to be absolutely certain of his loyalty—otherwise, they would be in trouble.

A woman opened the door to them. She looked familiar. Ellie realized she hadn't seen her before, but she wore the same traditional dress, her shoulders slumped and her gaze nearly empty.

"Joseph," she said. "Are you sure no one followed you?"

"Why would they? I have been questioned, and they let me go. They will let most of the others go soon."

"But not all of them. I knew Daniel was a fool getting involved with thugs."

Ellie cast a glance at the man who had appeared from the side—he had to be in his seventies. His white hair and beard gave him the impression of a gentle Santa Claus. She wasn't fooled. Jeremiah Deane was the man who had started the Prophets of Better Days, mapped out the idea in the first place.

Marrying young teens.

"I'm Ellie, Lilly's sister," she said, extending her hand. "You must be Jeremiah."

He frowned at the way she addressed him like she'd known he would. *Take that, I'm not waiting for your permission.* "You said I could see Lilly?"

"Yes, certainly. Come on in. I would like to sit down with you for a moment first."

"Why? Is she okay?"

"Lilly is fine. I just want to make sure you understand."

"I understand fine," Ellie said impatiently, keeping in character. "She went to join you, I only heard from her sporadically, and then nothing at all. Forgive me if that worries me."

"Like I said, you'll be able to talk to her soon. Come with me. Joseph?"

Joseph followed them wordlessly to a door at the end of a small hallway. Jeremiah unlocked it and gestured for Ellie to step inside the office space. She couldn't help being impressed. Within a few hours, the Prophets of Better Days, or what was left of them, had set up here. A laptop sat on a wooden desk, a shelf holding mostly folders.

"Son, you know what to do."

Ellie flinched as Joseph stepped behind her. "What does that mean?"

"We've had a few unfortunate incidents lately," Jeremiah explained. "We believe in the best of people, but the favor isn't always repaid, so we must remain cautious. I have to make sure you're not wearing a wire."

"A...what? I came here to see my sister!"

"Then you won't mind if we assure ourselves."

"I don't need help," she said, exasperated, and pulled her shirt over her head. The men waited in silence. She opened the zipper of her skirt next and let it fall to the floor. "Oh, for Pete's sake." When there was once again no reaction, she reached behind herself to open her bra.

"That's enough," Jeremiah said, holding up a hand. "You may cover yourself."

"Thank you." She made sure the sarcasm in her tone was unmistakable. Good job, Ellie, she told herself. She wasn't shaking on the outside. Inside was another story. This encounter was every bit as unsettling as she'd imagined. Unreal.

"You are welcome. How old are you, Ellie?"

For a moment she thought she had to be mistaken. Then again, this wasn't even surprising from someone who saw themselves above every criticism.

"I don't think that's any of your business. About Lilly?"

"Oh, sure. You may have dinner with us, and you can talk to Lilly after. Let's go."

They left through another door, and it wasn't until then that Ellie realized how big the building actually was. This wasn't some quickly put together operation. It was the Prophets' plan B.

There were about two dozen people sitting around a gigantic dining table, men, women, and children. The younger women were serving them.

Among the women sitting at the table was Lilah Strickland. Her eyes widened. Before she could react further, Ellie hurried to her side, pulling her up in a hug.

"Hey, sis, I'm so glad you're okay." She embraced her tightly, whispering, "Do they know?"

Lilah answered with a slight shake of her head.

"Good. We're going to get you out."

"How did you get here?" Lilah asked out loud.

"Please, everyone sit down." Jeremiah raised his voice. "Let's welcome in our midst, Ellie, Lilly's sister."

"Welcome, Ellie," the family said in unison. Ellie could have sworn Lilah had to resist rolling her eyes. She knew she had. She sat on the empty chair next to Lilah and gave her what she hoped was an encouraging smile. The young agent smiled back at her tiredly.

"I'm grateful the family let me see you. When you didn't answer my texts, I became worried, especially with everything that's in the news right now..."

"And there'll be time for that later," Jeremiah decided. "Let's pray."

Ellie was struck at how everyone fell in line immediately, many of the women and children with anxious looks on their faces. She felt anxious too—she had to try and get Lilah in a room alone. As it turned out, she would have to have dinner first.

Chapter
Seventeen

Apparently, Ellie's assignment with Bethany would exceed a normal workday. Jordan couldn't fight the growing worry that something might not be going as planned. No one had heard from Bethany, and she wasn't calling back.

Still, Derek had found her theory sound after she'd shown him her findings: One of the women they'd interviewed immediately after the raid, eighteen-year-old Cathy Deane, had been married to a cousin of Daniel Deane. Her maiden name was Biggs.

They caught the guard at the end of his shift.

"That was quick," he said. "You already found the murderer? I wasn't aware how fast those lab techs worked these days."

"Mr. Biggs, we have a few more questions. About your sister, Cathy." Jordan could tell from his expression that he had made the connection. "Do you know where she is?" she asked.

Even though Cathy could technically decide on her own where to live, her parents had come to collect her. On the compound, social workers had assisted the women who were forced to depend on their husbands for every decision—now that those men weren't there anymore, some of them were hopelessly overwhelmed. Not all of them had a family to go back to.

"Yes. She's at our parents'. I went to visit her, but...She's like an empty shell. That's what they do to them."

"People react differently to trauma."

"They turn them into robots. Every resistance, every bit of personality, they beat it out of them, and they 'marry' teenage girls to those old farts. I read quite a bit about groups like them. It's all about the power trip."

"I'm really sorry. Raphael Deane couldn't hurt anyone though."

"Not anymore, after he killed the woman who wrote the book."

"I understand you were angry."

"Yes. I was. Are you going to arrest me, or read me my rights?"

"Like my colleague said, we want to talk," Derek clarified. "If you work with us, there are options."

"Options, huh?" Biggs laughed bitterly. "I'll make it easy on you. Yes, I killed that son of a bitch. He deserved it. They all deserve it. You think time in prison will change them? They just believe harder that they are above everyone else."

"That's not the solution," Jordan told him as she put the cuffs on him.

"Really? Then what is?"

Some days, she didn't have all the answers.

❦

Ellie was well aware of Jeremiah watching her unabashedly.

"I missed you," she said to Lilah, earning a scolding look from the man who sat across from her. They didn't like dinner talk, especially from women. "They said I could talk to you alone later. I'd really like to know how you've been, and how you got here. Is this where you've been living all along?"

"There was a misunderstanding, and we had to leave the main house for a while," Lilah said cautiously. "It will all be okay. You told Mom where you were going? You should leave soon, so she doesn't worry."

Even in the tense situation, Ellie couldn't suppress the smile as she assumed mom was code for Bethany.

"But I just got here! I'd like to talk to you for a bit. Maybe you can show me around after dinner? This seems like a cool place."

"Later, okay?"

Lilah cast a soft smile in Jeremiah's direction.

"I apologize, I haven't even thanked you yet. It means a lot to me to see Ellie. Would you mind if I show her the house? I don't think she can stay long."

"Oh, but Joseph will be here for a while. She's welcome to stay for as long as he's here. Maybe you want to go to your room for a bit? You may do your chores after."

"Thank you so much."

The way he spoke to her, like to a child, made Ellie's stomach churn, but she forced a smile as well.

"I'd love to see your room." Ellie noticed that when they got up, the man from across got up as well and followed them. "Just checking if we're going where we said we were?" she whispered to Lilah who shrugged.

"Come. It's right here."

She closed the door behind them. The man remained standing outside. Ellie took a deep breath. At least they had made the right choice to wire Joseph instead of her.

She was going to say something, then thought twice about it and leaned close instead. "Bugged?"

"No," Lilah said, almost amused. "They couldn't have set it up that quickly. We just have to be quiet, because that guy outside the door is not moving."

"This is bigger than I expected," Ellie commented.

"Yeah. This place is huge. There are only a few of the Prophets left now, so I guess they didn't bother cramming the women into the tiny rooms like they did at the compound." Lilah laughed self-consciously. "I hope I'm not jinxing anything by talking about this like it's in the past."

"It will be soon. I know things haven't gone quite as planned, but this is almost over. They're waiting for the sign, and now that we're in here, Joseph will give it. Can you lock the door?"

"Joseph?"

"Yeah. He's working with us. The guy I came in with? You must know him?"

"Wow. Yes. Of course I do. I don't trust him."

"Dr. Roberts thinks he's okay. They made me strip as he predicted, so he was wearing the wire..."

Lilah shook her head. "No. Ellie, you need to get out of here right now. I can't—"

She broke off when the door opened, and the man in question walked in.

"Hey. You two are having a nice conversation, that's good. So, you're learning all about our family, Ellie. I'm glad."

Had Joseph lied to them? If that was the case, what would happen? Ellie realized that he was wearing a gun. There was no way Bethany would have let him go in like this, so one of the men must have given it to him.

What was his agenda?

"Now the family's all complete. Lilly told me that your mother is sick, so I guess she won't be able to come, but since you're here...You're invited, Ellie. I would like you to stay until the wedding."

"What is going on?" Ellie asked, confused for a moment. "We need to notify...now would be a good time."

"Oh, I don't know about that. Some things are better re-solved without outsiders. This won't keep them away forever, but it buys us some time." He opened his shirt to reveal the wire was gone.

"Please, don't panic. No one will get hurt. It was never our intention for anyone to get hurt, but unfortunately, there were a couple of black sheep in the family. They're taken care of now. We can all get on with our lives, and Lilly—Lilah—and I can finally move forward. Right, love?"

Lilah shook her head. "I'm sorry, Joseph. This will be over in a few hours, either way. I'm not going to marry you."

He looked shocked, and Ellie questioned the wisdom of Lilah's words, until she realized how close she was standing to him...and the gun in the holster.

"But...Jeremiah told me he isn't interested in you, because you've been on the outside for too long."

Ellie, while feeling sick about the implications of his words, focused on the matter at hand, stepping slightly closer while Joseph's whole attention was on Lilah.

"And I want to be on the outside," Lilah said. "With you. We don't need anyone's permission. Neither of us really wants this lifestyle, so why don't we just go away?"

"But we can't. We'd be giving up too much. Can't you see? Seth, Raphael, they all screwed up. Most of my brothers and cousins are in jail right now. I'm going to be the one to take over, soon. Once we get past Jeremiah, we—"

He spun around, but Ellie was already holding the gun in her hands.

"Where is that wire?"

"Oh, come on, don't be ridiculous. You know that without me, you'll never make it out of the house, or this room even.

Jeremiah trusts me. He knows about the wire—it's in his office now. They are preparing a retreat."

They all heard the first round of gunfire, and then it was returned. Screams ensued. Joseph had kept the FBI waiting for too long. He hadn't given the sign—now they were coming in.

"You need me," he insisted.

"Yeah, but it's too bad you can't be trusted. It looks like we're going to be better off without you."

The door was pushed open, and the man who had previously guarded the door, yelled at Joseph.

"Traitor!" He fired one shot, hitting Joseph, before Ellie pulled the trigger. The man staggered and fell back, clutching his arm. Lilah jumped to the man's side and picked up his gun.

"Flesh wound," she said, then she turned to Joseph who lay unmoving on the floor. Ellie noticed the expression on Lilah's face, something that seemed to go beyond any legitimate emotion either of them should have right now.

Before she could make any decision about what to do next, they heard rapid footsteps in the hallway. Ellie saw two women, most of them barely twenty, with young children. Some of them were crying.

"It's okay," she said. "I'm with the police. The FBI will be here any moment. You'll be safe."

She ushered all of them into the room where Lilah, the man's gun beside her, was still tending to Joseph.

There was still gunfire outside and around the house. "Let's barricade the door," Ellie said quickly. "Table, chairs, the dresser. Just to make sure no one comes in that isn't supposed to."

The women complied. One of them stared at the man Ellie had shot. "I need a doctor," he insisted. "You will all pay for this, and it won't be pretty."

Ellie followed the woman's gaze from the man to the gun at Lilah's side, and she made the connection right away.

"Don't," she whispered. "You want him to go away, not become a martyr."

The woman looked doubtful. Having learned details about what life was like for women and girls with the Prophets, she could sympathize—but she wanted this woman to be able to heal, not go to prison.

Ariel came to mind, and what she might have endured, had she stayed with the cult a few months longer. A year or two.

"It will be okay," she whispered, turning the woman by her shoulders so she wouldn't face the man anymore.

She cast a look over to where Lilah still sat hunched over Joseph, trying to stop the bleeding. Why had he played that game? Maybe some of the details in this case would forever remain a mystery.

***

Biggs sat in the interrogation room, his shoulders slumped, as he related how Cathy had become a member of the Prophets of Better Days. "I didn't know at first," he said. "She had some drug problems as a teenager but had been clean for many years. Cathy was always trying to find herself. When she joined them, I thought they were some sort of New Age kind of cult, and that she'd outgrow it...but then I realized they were violent to the women, brainwashing them. They have many children, but there is no love in those families. All they want is to produce soldiers for a culture war they imagine themselves to be in. If this guy hadn't told me..."

"What guy?"

Until now, Biggs hadn't mentioned any sort of accomplice.

"He came to visit Raphael, and we started talking. He had grown up in the cult but left it as a teenager. He was functioning as some sort of liaison, a consultant to the FBI or something."

He shrugged. "I don't blame him. I think he had a lot of anger for them too."

"What's his name?"

"Joseph. When he told me all the things that were going on in that place, I knew I needed to do something. I couldn't think straight..."

Son of a bitch. She almost said it out loud but held back the slur at the last moment. Bethany's mystery witness had apparently encouraged Biggs to commit homicide.

"Why don't you call your lawyer, and we take it from there?" she suggested, getting up. Biggs' case was pretty much cut and dry, but she didn't want the instigator to get away, especially if he might be involved with what Bethany and Ellie were doing at the moment.

"That's an odd moment to leave it," Valerie Esposito remarked when Jordan exited the room.

"Not at all. This guy, Joseph, that's the mystery witness. I need to know where Bethany is."

"If she doesn't tell you, I guess you have to ask her boss?"

"There's something else I can try first," Jordan said.

Sergeant Bristol confirmed that Bethany hadn't given him many details as to Ellie's assignment.

"This changes things," he said. "Let me make a few calls."

"Thank you, sir."

Chapter Eighteen

I t seemed like an eternity since the agents on the other side of the door had identified themselves, and Ellie, Lilah and their charges could finally start to dismantle their makeshift barricade.

The women left the room with their children. Sarah, who had nearly reached for the gun, turned around and embraced Ellie.

"Thank you," she whispered before she left with the others.

Bethany walked inside. Ellie saw that her hair was slightly disheveled, and there was a smear of blood on her face. None of that did impede her, though.

"God, I'm so glad we can finally clean this up. This was the last of it, huh? Welcome home, Agent Strickland. You did an extraordinary job."

Lilah gave her a distant smile while she was still applying pressure to Joseph's gunshot wound.

"We have to keep him alive," she said. "I believe he hasn't told us the whole story yet."

A couple of paramedics came inside, taking over for Lilah who got to her feet, her hands wet with blood.

"Ellie did good too."

For a moment, Ellie had wondered if she, too, deserved some praise, but she'd decided it wasn't all that important. The emotion in Bethany's expression was telling—she wasn't that cold. She truly cared about the young agent.

Ellie followed the two of them at a distance, tired but relieved. She was finally able to answer a question that had been haunting her since the shootout with Seth Deane.

She hadn't folded under pressure. She had reacted when she had to. Still, Ellie hoped she wouldn't have to shoot her weapon again for a long time to come.

Jordan was standing with Derek and Kate at his desk when Ellie returned to the precinct. She went straight into Jordan's embrace.

"It's so good to see you. You have no idea."

"Same here," Jordan said.

"I'm sorry. There was no time to—"

"I know. It's okay. If the FBI pulls you in on a case, you can't say no. I understand."

Ellie looked surprised, probably listening for a trace of sarcasm, but there was none. Jordan was happy to see her, no hidden meaning.

"And so, once again, Roberts has a mess to clean up after the fact," Derek summed up the situation.

"Well, everything is a lot clearer now. Joseph told us that Jeremiah had ordered Raphael to kill Jennifer, and that he's also responsible for Deborah's death," Ellie reminded him.

"Does that mean the end justifies every means?" Derek asked.

"God! I'm so sick of this," Kate snapped. "Why don't you ask her out, since you're so preoccupied with her all the damn time?"

"I'm not—" Derek didn't have enough time for his defense as Kate jumped to her feet and walked away. After a moment of startled hesitation, he followed her. When Bethany entered the room at the same time Derek left, they didn't acknowledge each other.

"Are you really not mad at me?" Ellie asked into the resulting silence.

In the past two days, Jordan had struggled to name her feelings. Anger might have been one of them, but it wasn't directed at Ellie.

"No. I'm the only person she's mad at," Bethany, who had overheard her words, said.

That anger wasn't even directed at her ex.

"I never said that."

Bethany shrugged. "You didn't have to. I know you well enough, but that's okay. I just came to say goodbye. We've had some glitches, but this really is the end of the Prophets and their megalomaniac bullshit."

"You're leaving?" Ellie asked and then looked a bit self-conscious, as if her reaction was a too happy one.

It was a relief, Jordan admitted. They could put their differences aside to work together, but there would always be tension.

"Yes. I received some stern words, but it wasn't enough for a change of plans. The Powers That Be are very happy to have one less trigger-happy women-hating bunch to worry about. With the sentences most of them are likely to get, it will be enough for the women to start over."

When the reaction she got, obviously wasn't enough, Bethany pulled a chair, sitting across from Jordan.

"We got them all. You can't tell me it wasn't worth it."

"I didn't say anything."

"I was well within my competence. Ellie knew the case well enough, and she was someone Lilah would recognize right away."

"Sergeant Bristol said so, and I suppose your boss would confirm it. Congratulations on your promotion."

"Thank you." Bethany seemed relieved too. "I couldn't have done this without you guys, and I'm really grateful. Ellie, good luck on your exam."

"Thanks." Ellie waited until Bethany had left, then she said, "Did I miss something?"

Jordan sighed. "No. I swear. We've been over this often enough, and yes, I wanted to yell at her, but what good would that do? Bristol signed off on the assignment. I don't ever want you to be in danger, but I'm not going to stop you from doing your job, from having a career. I promise." Much to her credit, Ellie didn't look surprised at all. She leaned into Jordan.

"I know," she said.

"And I want to start looking for a place together, but I admit there was no time yet to look for a realtor."

"That's because you solved a case within a few hours. Way to go."

"Well, there has to be something we can still teach you once you move up to our floor," Jordan teased. "Otherwise, you could just skip the whole exam and everything."

"I love you, but this talk is going to make you sleep on the couch. I'm nervous enough about it, so no joking."

"The couch is fine. Not so much privacy, but I'll show you how I can work with the space."

Ellie shook her head, laughing. "I'm so glad this is over."

"Yeah, me too. Let's go home?"

⟨⟩

It didn't look like Kate was going to come home tonight. Maybe they hadn't even spared that much rational thought because the couch was right there when they stumbled into the apartment kissing, starting to undress each other.

The celebration ended abruptly when they heard the key in the lock, and Kate walked inside, in a stormy mood.

"What's wrong with your bedroom?"

A moment later, the bathroom door slammed shut, and Ellie sat up, reality catching up with her. Kate had been morose and tight-lipped for a few days now. Ellie had meant to talk to her, but then they hardly saw each other alone, and there was so much to do...

She slipped her shirt back on.

"Did you talk to her about...the plans?" Jordan asked softly.

"No, not yet. I don't know what's going on...but I'll find out."

"I can pick you up for breakfast tomorrow," Jordan suggested, buttoning her shirt.

Ellie stilled her hands. "Wait, you missed one. No, it's fine, please, stay. I just want to check on her."

"Okay."

Ellie gently knocked on the door. At first, there was no answer.

"Kate, come on. Let's talk."

"Can't you just leave me alone for a moment?"

"Please, open the door."

Kate finally did, but when Ellie stepped inside, she sat back down against the tub.

Ellie sat down in front of her, realizing her friend had been crying.

"Talk to me. I know I haven't been a good friend lately, but I'm here now. I promise I'll do better."

Kate leaned forward, covering her face with her hands.

"It's not your fault. You've had a full plate for some time now."

Yes, and add to that the new moving plans. This was definitely not a good time to reveal them.

"We both have," Ellie ventured. Life always went on, it had to, and on the surface, they were okay...but she knew Kate was still dealing with nightmares of her own. "You and Derek are all right?"

Kate made a non-committal sound. "We've always been as all right as we possibly can be, given the circumstances. I...I miss Jensen."

"That's only normal. I'm sure Derek understands."

"Yeah, that's the problem, he's too damn understanding about everything. Oh, no, forget I said that. It's not fair. I'm not even sure I can look at any of this in a way that's fair, but Ellie, it's too much."

Ellie scooted closer to embrace her friend.

"I know you were deeply invested in this case. We all were. Maybe you need a break too."

Kate sat back, giving her an intent look.

"I don't think so."

"What do you mean?"

"A break is not going to do it. I just want it over. I thought I could move on, like everyone else, but it's not happening. Every day, I'm reminded that it could happen again, to someone I care about. I don't want to live with that. I don't want that anymore."

Ellie needed a few seconds to absorb what Kate was saying. She hadn't realized how different she and Kate were in that respect. Even with everything that had happened in the past months, leaving the force was nothing that had ever occurred to her as a realistic solution. She was sure Jordan felt the same, even if she did deal in ways different from Ellie's.

But maybe, for Kate, it was a decision she needed to make.

"Many of your friends are still going to be cops...and Derek will be," she reminded her.

"I'm aware of that," Kate said with a wry laugh. "Maybe I'm selfish enough, and I'll be all right if I'm not confronted with the possibility every day. Maybe I should stop dating cops."

"What would you like to do instead? Job-wise, I mean?"

"You're the first I'm telling this, and obviously, I haven't given a lot of thought to the details yet. But I might go back to school. I used to want to become a lawyer."

"Are you really sure about this?"

"Leaving? Yes. I think it's the right choice. But I'm sorry for snapping at you."

"That's okay," Ellie ascertained. "We should have expected you to come home at some point."

"Well, we're grown-ups. I could have been less of a bitch. Could you say sorry to Jordan for me? I need to wash my face, and I need some time to figure everything out. Thanks for listening."

"No problem. Are you sure you're okay?"

"That's relative...but I'll be fine. Go."

"Okay. And remember I'm here if you need me."

As she left the bathroom, Ellie remembered she had made that promise to someone else as well, and just as with Kate, she'd been too busy. Tomorrow, she'd redeem herself. Tomorrow, she was going to see Ariel.

Chapter
Nineteen

J ordan felt a lot more confident in her decisions these days, career-wise and when it came to her relationship with Ellie. She had called a realtor first thing in the morning, then brewed some coffee and gone to the bakery down the street to get some fresh pastries for breakfast. Kate had left early.

When Jordan returned to the apartment, Ellie was still asleep, so she kissed her awake softly.

"Hey. I smell something delicious. It's not a special day?"

Given what they'd been through, every day truly was a special day, but Jordan didn't want to dampen the mood with a reminder.

"You like breakfast before going to work," she said. "It's ready."

Ellie got to her feet and walked into the kitchen where the table was set for two.

"I could get used to this," she admitted, and Jordan embraced her from behind.

"Me too."

Jordan spent the morning piecing together her report for the case she had solved within in a few hours. She was careful not to step on any toes regarding the FBI's secret witness, who wasn't such a mystery any longer. Joseph's statement partly supported Lilah's, though it still wasn't entirely clear why he had tried to play both sides and removed the wire. He was still in the hospital, recovering from the gunshot wound.

Jeremiah had given the order to kill Jennifer—because of the book.

And, according to Joseph, he had killed Deborah to stop her from fleeing the cult. He hadn't gone after Ariel...no time? He had other plans for her? The thought made her shudder.

At the hospital, she had been able to interview him briefly about the murder of Raphael Deane before the FBI took over.

Jeremiah Deane had denied knowing about Deborah's plan to leave the cult.

Something didn't add up. Joseph might have once been the mystery witness—ironically, much about him still was a mystery.

Jordan made a few calls, learning that he already had been transferred to the infirmary of the jail where he would be held until the trial.

There were a few more questions that needed answers.

"Detective? I'm surprised to see you," he said when she introduced herself. "I'm not sure I can help you. I've been working with the FBI."

"I'm aware. There are a couple of details I'd like to go over with you."

He looked pale but alert. "Really? What's left?"

"You saw Jeremiah Deane kill Deborah."

"That's what I said."

"You know we've been over at the house, looking at the scene. It's possible. You had a fairly good angle to see what was going on. Why didn't you help?"

"Come on, Detective, I answered that too. You don't go up against the brothers, at least not face to face. This is why I co-operated with the FBI right away. They sent me in to talk to some of the members, carefully convince them to talk, and in the end, establish contact with Jeremiah."

"But then it wasn't as clean as it could have been, had you stuck to the plan."

Jordan might have no good reason to be angry with Bethany, but she was angry with him. He had played both sides and risked a lot of lives that day.

"What are you getting at? I told you already that whatever the guard made of my story, it's not my fault he became a killer. As for Deborah, like Jennifer, Jeremiah wanted to keep her from talking. He trusted that most of the women would be too scared of losing their children, and the lawyers would get the men out soon enough."

"What was your long-term plan in all this? You wanted to marry Lilah Strickland? Or maybe you had an interest in Deborah as well? And other women before her?"

"You're wrong," he said angrily. "Dead wrong."

"Am I? I understand that there's a pretty disgusting hierarchy in these cults. You don't get to have your multiple wives right away. You have to work for it, and the brothers don't like sharing all that much. That's what you told Biggs. Young girls who were born into the cult, or runaways off the street, they all belong to them first, and they decide who can marry, and how many. Why aren't you married, Joseph?"

"I was going to marry soon."

"Who, Lilah Strickland? That was part of her cover. If one of the brothers allowed for you to court her, that meant she was as safe as she could possibly be among you. And you're pretty old to get started. What did you do to piss off the brothers?"

"What the hell are you talking about? They liked me. They trusted me!" He struggled into a more upright position.

"I think they wouldn't let you marry, so you had to find something on them. Blackmail them, even threaten to...wait, work with the FBI?"

"You have no idea what you're saying. You have no idea who you're talking to."

Something was changing about his demeanor. Jordan had seen that expression before, the glee in his eyes. It startled her to see it in a man who had successfully positioned himself as a double agent for quite some time.

"I think I'm beginning to," she said. Jordan left the room and, after a moment of hesitation, called Bethany.

"I didn't think I would see you again," Ariel said matter-of-fact-ly, and Ellie couldn't blame her.

"I called ahead and told Mrs. Milner that I was going to bring lunch."

"Oh, lucky me. Finally, I can watch TV and eat junk food like all the other kids."

Ariel's tone said clearly that she believed she'd never be like all the other kids, and given her experiences, she might be right.

"I am sorry it took me so long. You know that some members of the group escaped during the first raid, and when we found them, I was helping out."

"It's okay. The detective—Jordan—was here, with the A.D .A. I'll still need to testify, right?"

"I'm afraid so, but we'll do the best to shield you from any cult members."

The girl shrugged. "They were around all my life, and I know they will hate me. That's fine. I hate them for what they did to my mom, and I want them to be held responsible. I'll do anything I can."

"We will help you, I promise. How are you doing?"

"Mrs. Milner is nice, but I know I won't be able to stay here."

"Yeah. There's going to be a place more permanent for you. It will all work out."

"Is that what people told you after your parents died?"

"Some, and I didn't want to hear it at the time. I had friends to help me through that time."

"Good for you."

"You have friends, too," Ellie told her.

After she left, she took a turn outside of the city to go to a place she had rarely gone to lately. She walked through the rows, startled at how the cemetery had grown since her last visit. She remembered coming for Jensen Baker's funeral. She remembered the other funeral, all those years ago, where she'd been so doped up she was barely conscious. She hadn't been able to escape the pain in the long run.

"Hey Mom and Dad," she whispered after laying down a bouquet of flowers, thinking it was silly, because she didn't even believe in a presence, right here. It was mostly a painful reminder. "So much has happened since the last time." Ellie brushed her hand over the names engraved in the headstone, Meredith Evans-Harding and Patrick Harding.

She wasn't quite ready to leave yet when her phone vibrated in the pocket of her pants, but seeing the call came from Jordan, she answered it.

"Hey."

"Where are you? Still on break?"

"Yes. What happened?"

"I suppose you'll hear it on the radio in a minute, but I thought I could reach you. We are turning the compound upside down."

Ellie didn't understand right away. "Why? I thought...Wait. What did you find?"

"Bones," Jordan said somberly. "As if what the brothers started wasn't vile enough...they also covered up the sick compulsion of one of their sons. There was a reason Joseph wasn't married."

Ellie's stomach turned. "Oh my God."

"He couldn't care less that Deborah and Jennifer wanted to expose the Prophets of Better Days. He wanted all the glory—well, that, and many brides."

"I'm on my way," Ellie said.

❧

Bethany's goodbye had been a bit premature, as they now had to deal with the graveyard uncovered underneath the basement of the schoolhouse.

Being right wasn't always a reason to be happy, but at least they'd be able to provide closure to even more families now. The crew had uncovered four bodies, proving the brothers to be guilty of even more crimes than they had originally imagined.

Instead of turning Joseph over to the authorities, they had covered for him, every time an "accident" happened. Finally, he revealed that he had been willing to leave Jennifer to Raphael, because he liked her. Somewhere along the line, when he realized that the Prophets not only wouldn't send a lawyer but were either in jail or on the run themselves, Raphael freaked out. He was planning to tell the whole story, and so Joseph put Plan B in motion.

Jordan and Derek were both working at their respective desks. Ellie had texted her that she'd be there in a few minutes.

They'd go home and change, go to a restaurant or join some colleagues at the *Night Shift*. Everyone was overdue for a break.

She realized that would have to wait when she saw the man in the cheap suit coming her way. Jordan recognized him right away. Self-preservation was part of it.

"Counselor, how are you today?" Part of her hoped that the sarcasm might reach him. She didn't hold her breath.

"Ms. Carpenter...Excuse me, Detective."

Jordan was sure he had done it on purpose. She was aware of Derek watching them, shaking her head in his direction. She could handle the sleazy lawyer on her own.

"I'm off at this moment. So please, don't bother."

"I'm here on behalf of Mr. Darby."

"I imagined. That's why you shouldn't bother. I have nothing to say to him, and I'm not going to participate in one of his games. Goodnight, Mr. Donovan."

"He knows you're not going to talk to him, so he asked me to give you this." He held up a white envelope. "Don't worry," Donovan added with a nervous laugh. "It's been cleared. Nothing dangerous in there."

"Yeah, but why would you think I care?"

"Detective, Mr. Darby is a very sick man."

Jordan let out a wry laugh. "No kidding."

In her opinion, this conversation was already going on too long. In person or writing, she didn't want any contact with the worst nightmare of her life. Or maybe it had taken second place when Ellie was kidnapped. In any case, she was over it.

The attorney placed the envelope onto her desk.

"I know what you're thinking, but this might be helpful for you too. If you can make anything of it...It's all about control, right, isn't that what psychiatrists say?"

"Go, before I come up with something to have you arrested."

"I'm sorry. Detective. I happen to believe that everyone deserves representation, no matter what they've done. You won't have to worry about Mr. Darby much longer. He's dying."

"In that case I take back what I said. This is the best news I've gotten all day. Thanks for stopping by."

Fortunately, he got the message. "Please understand I had to do this on behalf of my client. You have a good evening." He turned around and left, nodding to Ellie, who had just returned. She headed straight to Jordan's desk.

"What did he want?" she asked, the tone of her voice revealing that she, too, had recognized Donovan.

Jordan shrugged. "Bring me a letter from Darby. Apparently, he's terminally ill, so he's trying to play everyone one last time. I won't fall for it."

"You're not curious?"

"Not one bit. Are you ready?" Her tone was a bit sharper than intended.

"Sure. Let me just talk to Derek for a second. I have a message from Kate."

"Okay. I'll be waiting outside. I think I need some fresh air."

A few moments later, on the steps of the precinct, Jordan took a deep breath. She was certain that this was the right decision. She had made the mistake seeking out Darby when Ellie got mysterious text messages, and he had tried to get into her head again, almost succeeded. The world would be better off without him, no doubt. He had brought pain to many. With individuals like him, it was hard to take the high road and stay on it, not wish exactly the same for him.

Either way, she never had to see him again. Especially on a day like this, with all the horrors uncovered, Jordan was grateful for that fact.

She'd see her new realtor tomorrow—time to look to the future.

"You don't have a message for me, do you?" Derek observed as Ellie bent down to retrieve the crumpled paper from the wastepaper basket, calling her bluff. "You're sure this is a good idea?"

"No," Ellie admitted. "But someday she might change her mind and want to know."

"You'll keep it until then?"

"No. I'll tell her soon."

Derek shrugged in a way that said, "You must know."

Ellie was fairly convinced that she did. She caught up with Jordan outside of the precinct, linking her arm with Jordan's.

"I'm starving. I think I don't feel like a lot of company tonight. Just the two of us, a bottle of wine and some take-out, how does that sound?"

Jordan kissed her softly.

"That sounds perfect," she whispered.

About the Author

B arbara Winkes writes sapphic crime drama and Christmas romance. She loves writing characters who get the job done, whether it's stopping a predator or saving cherished traditions—while still making time for love. She lives with her wife in Quebec City.

barbarawinkes.com

Also by Barbara Winkes

The Crossing Lines Trilogy
Undercover
Redemption
Vengeance

The Connected Series
Promised to the Queen
Drawn to the Enemy
Tempted by the Protector

Kelli & Merin Romantic Suspense
Thunder
Rain

Standalone
The Amnesia Project